# WHEN *Love* CHIMES

# WHEN *Love* CHIMES

## A Broken Valor Novel

# LEXI POST

USA TODAY & NY TIMES BESTSELLING AUTHOR

# SUMMARY

He's the right man at the wrong time with an unwanted Christmas proposal.

As if cocktail waitress and horse trainer Lynzie Mullins didn't have enough problems, she discovers she's pregnant just as her high school crush rides back into town in time for Christmas. He's a constant reminder of the happily ever after she'd always dreamed of instead of the mess she's in now.

Cowboy veteran Ryan Crawford reluctantly returns to Lucasville to help his grandpa sell his place. The town has changed and so has Lynzie—from an awkward teenager to an attractive young woman with a caring heart.

Despite his best efforts, Lynzie's not interested in leaving Lucasville, so Ryan offers her what she wants—his heart. Unfortunately, that proves not to be enough. Now he has a decision to make. Give up his dream farm or his dream girl.

# ACKNOWLEDGMENTS

For Bob Fabich, my own dream man. Thank you for all the meals at my desk and for giving up your time with me while I wrote this story.

And for my sister Paige Wood, who made the best Thanksgiving dinner ever and still found time to beta read this story at the last minute. A special shout out to Brian Wood, my brother-in-law, who came through once again with a title, this one the title for the *Broken Valor* series.

A huge thank you to my critique partner, Marie Patrick, who has been so patient with me in waiting for my critiques of her work while she works on mine. Also, thank you to John Warner, Marie's wonderful husband, for his expert mechanic's advice. No one knows the inner workings of a vehicle better than John.

Lastly, I'd like to thank Liz Crowe for creating such a unique world as Lucasville and the Love Brothers, and for allowing me to enter it.

# AUTHOR'S NOTE

*When Love Chimes* is a "bridge" book. It is the first book in the *Broken Valor* series and the prequel to *Desires of Christmas Present: A Christmas Carol Book #2.* *When Love Chimes* was inspired by a Christmas story by Charles Dickens known as "The Chimes," but the full title is "The Chimes: A Goblin Story of Some Bells that Rang an Old Year Out and a New Year In." In his story, Dickens' main character, Trotty, a poor ticket-porter, is told by those with more wealth that his and his daughter Meg's existence is doomed to evil and the world would be better without them. Meg is swayed by one while Trotty is swayed by many and Meg decides not to go through with marrying the man she loves.

Feeling worthless, Trotty, who works beneath the bells every day, goes out that night and climbs the tower. The spirits of the tower decide to teach him a lesson and show him what accepting the viewpoint of the wealthy will do to his daughter. After being forced to watch Meg's life play out until she is at the brink of drowning herself and her unborn babe, Trotty begs the spirits to save her, having realized the error of his ways. He is allowed to touch her and keep her from jumping at the last second.

On New Year's Day morning, Trotty wakes in his own bed as if from a dream and finds Meg has decided to marry and their friends throw a wedding feast for the new couple. Dickens' obvious championship for the poor is easily followed in this story.

What if a similar philosophy was found in today's world and the new rich in one area of an old town saw little use for the older, less wealthy inhabitants? Could two people who always loved each other find eventual happiness or would the interference and attitudes of the "transplants" destroy all hope? It may just take a tragedy and a little help from a very special source just like the spirits of the chimes.

# CHAPTER ONE

I'm pregnant." Lynzie Mullins stared at the word "yes" on the home pregnancy test-strip. Joy, fear, and anger collided inside her.

"Are you sure?" Her best friend, Coco Baker, grabbed the stick out of her hand. "Oh boy, that makes it pretty clear, but I've heard that you should get a real test done by a doctor. These aren't always accurate."

Lynzie took the stick back, still stunned. How could this have happened? Sure, she wanted children someday, but she'd like to have a husband first. Cocktail waitressing wasn't the most lucrative profession, and the only horse farm in town was falling apart, so training horses was out.

"You aren't going to tell him, are you?" Coco's question pulled her back from her worried thoughts.

"Who?"

Coco rolled her eyes. "Andrew. Who else? Unless you've been sleeping with someone other than him. I thought you guys use protection."

"We do." But she'd stopped taking the pill because of the expense. Besides, Andrew could afford the really good condoms. She flopped down on the couch. Would Andrew help with child support? Would he insist on a DNA test? How much would that cost? Maybe he'd ask her to marry him.

Who was she kidding? He was nice and he liked getting into bed with her, but she knew he considered himself above her. He came from the new section of Lucasville.

They had fun together. It wasn't as if they were in love and while she hadn't slept with anyone while with him, she was pretty sure he had a few other women he saw on a regular basis. A perk of having money.

Coco sat down next to her. "What are you going to do?" Her friend's eyes were honestly concerned. Coco had too soft a heart. She also had a weird ability to recognize people who were soulmates, though she never volunteered that information.

Maybe Lynzie should ask Coco if she and Andrew were soulmates, but she swore she'd never to do that. Everyone bothered Coco about that and as her best friend, she refused to do the same. Besides, she knew the answer already—no. "I don't know. I just found out. I'm still reeling a bit."

"A bit? If it was me, I think I'd faint." Coco laid back over the arm of the couch with the back of her hand on her forehead.

Lynzie smiled. She appreciated her friend trying to cheer her up. "I think I'll do what you said, go to a doctor. In the meantime, let's keep this between us."

Coco sat up and nodded. "Of course."

They sat in silence a few minutes, Lynzie still staring at the word "yes." It probably wasn't going to magically change to a "no" just because she wanted it to. Sighing, she rose and threw it away.

Coco crossed and re-crossed her legs. She didn't like silence very much. "Not to change the subject, but I'm guessing you won't mind too much if I do. Did you hear that Ryan Crawford came back to town last night?"

Lynzie's heart sped up at the very mention of her old high school crush. "No, I didn't hear."

Coco nodded. "According to Antony, Ryan has come back to help his grandpa sell his old horse farm. I haven't seen him yet, but I hear he looks a lot different."

Just great. "Why? Does he have a limp, burn scars, a big belly? He looked pretty good to me when we were in school."

Coco laughed. "You were the only one who thought so. I think you mixed up his kindness with his looks. That boy was a nerd before they even had a term for it."

She leaned on the counter separating her kitchenette from her living room. "He wasn't that bad. He didn't even wear glasses."

"Well, from what I hear, he's looking mighty fine now. I guess he went into the Army."

"Really? Now how did you find out about that if he just came in last night?"

Coco winked. "I ran into Margot and she said Ryan called Antony about some part-time work at the Love Garage. Want to take a walk and see if we bump into him? You don't have to work until later."

She must be an idiot because she actually considered Coco's idea. "No. I'm sure we'll connect eventually."

"Suit yourself."

If she'd suited herself, she would have run away with Ryan when he first left town. At this point in her life, she wasn't sure if she could handle meeting his wife and kids, if he had them. "Maybe I should—"

A knock at her door stopped her. She stood to answer it, and Coco put her finger to her lips. If it was Andrew, she'd keep the baby stuff to herself…until she'd had a doctor's visit.

She opened the door. "Hello?"

A man with dark hair and a white cowboy hat stood there filling out his blue t-shirt to its max, the outline of his pectorals clear as day. Her entire body took notice.

He smiled, his white teeth gleaming against his tan skin. "Hi, Lynzie."

Huh? A customer from the bar maybe? She would

have never missed such a hot hunk of a man. "I'm sorry, do I know you?"

"I hope so, it's me. Ryan Crawford."

She opened her mouth, but nothing came out. She couldn't stop herself from cataloging everything about him from his very short haircut, to his bulging biceps to the breadth of his chest. "Ryan Crawford?"

He grinned. "Yeah, I've been getting a lot of that today."

She returned her gaze to his mesmerizing eyes. "Oh, my God, Ryan!" She threw her arms around him, beyond thrilled. When his strong arms captured her against his chest, she gave in to the feel of his hard body pressed against her own.

As soon as he loosened his hold, she reluctantly stepped back, old feelings rushing through her. "It's so good to see you. Coco just told me you were in town, but even so, I would have walked right past you in the street and not have known it was you."

"Ahem." Coco cleared her throat.

"Oh, I'm sorry. Come in." She opened the door wider and let him walk by. He took his cowboy hat off and held it in both hands. She closed the door and stepped next to him. "Do you remember Coco Baker?"

He gave her friend a smirk. "How could I forget *hot* Coco."

Coco squinched her nose up at the old nickname

then looked at Lynzie before she cocked her head and studied Ryan from the top of his head to the bottom of his black cowboy boots. "My, my, have you changed."

He grimaced. "So I've heard." Then he grinned. "But you haven't much, though the pink streak in your hair makes me think of peppermint hot chocolate." He winked.

"Oh, come here and give me a hug." Coco wrapped her arms around Ryan, and Lynzie tensed. She shouldn't. Coco was her best friend and for all she knew, Ryan was married, but lost love died hard, at least for her.

When Coco stepped away, Ryan turned toward her. "I'm actually on my way to Antony's place, but I had to stop by and see you. You look good."

She felt her cheeks flush. She looked like crap in her ratty jeans and white tank. She'd thrown her hair up in a clip that morning and hadn't even brushed it. "Thanks. How long are you in town for? I heard you're going to work at the Love Garage."

He shrugged. "Not sure yet about either. Probably through the holidays. I'm helping Gramps get his old Lazy Acres farm ready to sell. It has really gone to h—heck. I figured I'd see if I couldn't bring in a little cash to help pay for repairs. All Gramps has now is his social security."

That was typical for the old locals of Lucasville.

"How great that you're doing that for him." *So, are you married? Do you want to move back here permanently? How do you feel about babies?*

"Lynzie?" Coco caught her off guard.

"What?"

Her friend rolled her eyes then looked at Ryan. "You'll have to excuse her. She didn't get much sleep last night."

That was the truth. "I'm sorry. What did you say?"

Ryan's dark brown eyes seemed to laugh at her. "I wanted to know if you have any time tonight to catch up."

"Oh." Her heart started jumping like a wild rabbit. "I would love—" Coco elbowed her in the side and shook her head. Now why wouldn't she be able to meet—Oh crap, she was scheduled at the pub. "I would love to, but I have to work. Days are better for me. Do you have any time tomorrow?"

Ryan nodded. "Sure. I doubt Antony will hire me on the spot, but they're really busy, so I'm guessing he will eventually. How about lunch tomorrow?"

She smiled. "Perfect."

"Great. I'll pick you up around one. I don't want to take a table for hours from a local business. We have a lot of catching up to do."

Now her heart was jumping harder than a kangaroo. "I'll be ready."

"See you then." Ryan nodded then looked at her

friend. "Coco." He set his hat back on his head and strode for the door.

She stood frozen to the spot until Coco pushed her towards him and she followed. As he stepped out into the sunshine, she held the door open. "Bye."

He gave her a quick smile of his own before descending the stairs to the parking lot below.

She really should close the door, but instead, she watched him until he jumped into a big white pick-up and backed out.

"Get back in here." Coco grabbed her arm and pulled her inside, shutting the door on the hot man that just re-entered her life.

She looked at her friend. "Oh my God, I can't believe he stopped by. Did you see him? He's gorgeous and built and totally sweet."

Coco laughed. "He sure is. That's one hot cowboy."

Lynzie fell back onto the couch. "His eyes are the same. I always loved his eyes."

"Right, his eyes." Coco chuckled. "So while you were looking at his eyes, I was looking at his hands."

"His hands?" She frowned. "I didn't notice them. Were they large?"

"Shoot, Lynzie. Come down off cloud nine for a minute. I looked at his hands to see if he had a wedding ring."

She hadn't even thought of that. Suddenly, tingles raced along her skin. "And?"

Coco's smile was smug. "Nope."

She inhaled deeply at the idea that Ryan might still be available then tried to calm down. "He could still be married and not wear a ring or he could have a serious girlfriend or even fiancée." But she really, really hoped he didn't.

Coco threw her hands up. "Could you stop being the pessimist for just a few minutes? Sometimes you drive me crazy with that."

She gave her friend a sheepish smile. "Sorry. Habit. Just too many of my dreams have been crushed. It's hard to have a positive outlook."

Coco dropped down next to her. "I know. I just think there might be hope this time."

She studied Coco, trying to decide if she knew more than she was letting on. Was Ryan her soulmate? She'd sworn she'd never ask. They were too close, and she didn't want to be like half the women in town, pestering Coco to find out if their latest boyfriend was *the one*. Or even going to the mall with her and asking if she could point out their soulmate.

Just as her hope started to rise, she crushed it with her new reality. "But I'm pregnant."

Even Coco's usual cheerful demeanor hesitated in light of that fact. "You don't know for sure. I suggest you make that doctor's appointment and quick."

Ryan parked down the street of the Love Garage, but didn't get out of his truck. He was still recovering from seeing Lynzie again. She'd matured, her gangly teenage body had filled out perfectly. She was still thin and tall, but she had some nice curves he hadn't been oblivious to when she hugged him.

Her face had grown even more beautiful, her green eyes with her naturally long lashes still captivated him. Her full cheeks had thinned, showing off prominent cheek bones, but her nose still had a little point at the end that made him want to kiss it. He was anxious to see how long her hair was. From what he could see, it was darker with less blonde highlights like maybe she wasn't outside as much as she used to be.

She had been the hardest part of leaving Lucasville. She'd also given him the best reception since he returned yesterday evening. Everyone treated him like a traitor or a liar. He wasn't sure which pissed him off more. He was sixteen when his mom divorced his dad and moved them to Florida to live with her parents. It wasn't like he had a choice. The way people in the older part of town were acting, it was as if he'd turned his back on them.

He gripped the steering wheel tighter. It was his father who turned his back on him and Gramps. His grandpa had to be pretty desperate to have contacted his mom and asked for help. The old man was losing it. He muttered to himself a lot and forgot what he was doing. What if he hadn't remembered he had a grandson?

Guilt crept up Ryan's back. For all the resentment he had for his father, he should have at least called his gramps. His mother wouldn't have done anything to keep the relationship going after what his dad had done to her, so he should have made an effort.

Cracking his neck to relieve the sudden tension, he released the wheel. He couldn't change the past, but he was here now and he needed some part-time work if he planned to bring Lazy Acres into saleable condition.

Jumping out of his truck, he walked toward the garage. There were cars parked outside, waiting their turn to be fixed while sounds of rivet guns and country music populated the air through the two open garage bays. The warm weather was an oddity. He would be freezing his ass off in Lucasville soon, especially after living in Florida for so long.

Walking into the chaos that was actually like a well-oiled engine, Ryan felt his blood race. The smell of oil and sight of cars up on lifts reminded him of his days in the Army where working on trucks and tanks had been his oasis…until the day he was wounded.

Still, the sights, sounds and smells of a garage had his hands itching to get dirty.

"Morning, we're pretty slammed today. What's the problem?"

Ryan stifled his grin. Having no one recognize him was getting old, but looking at Antony Love, he couldn't help playing with the man. "Well, I'm pretty sure the transmission is blown. When I shift gears, it's obvious third and fourth isn't working right. Plus, I need new rotors and brake pads, an oil change and my steering wheel is shot."

Antony stared at him, probably counting up the hours and the money it would cost to take care of all those problems. "What kind of car did you say you had?"

"A 1969 GT350 Mustang." He'd always wanted one of those, until he had a chance to drive a tank. Now *that* was real power.

"You're fucking with me. No one in this town has one of those. I'd know."

"Who said I was from here?" Ryan shrugged. "Okay, maybe I'm *from* here, but I just got back."

Antony scowled. "You ass. Ryan Crawford, do you really own a GT350 or are you just making me drool?"

"Just making you drool. But I figured it'd make you happy to know I don't own one either."

Antony shook his head. "Just what I need, a lying mechanic." He studied him another minute but no warm handshake was coming. "Come this way, let's see what you've got. What garage experience do you have?"

"Six years in the Army."

Antony's step hesitated for a second, but he kept walking. "What'd you work on?"

"Mostly Tanks, Strykers and Cougars. A few jeeps here and there, but I fixed pretty much anything they threw at me, including a Black Hawk that wouldn't lift off with a belly full of wounded."

This time Antony did stop and face him. "Overseas?"

He nodded. "Afghanistan."

Antony didn't say anything, but something in his demeanor shifted. Ryan just hoped it was in his favor. There wasn't much else he could do for work if he couldn't work on vehicles. From what'd he'd seen, there weren't any horse farms left in the area that he could hire onto.

They walked over to a small old pick-up truck up on the lift. From the looks of things, the mechanic working on it had just replaced the brake pads. He stepped out from under the vehicle as Antony approached. "I've looked at this thing from front to back and I can't find any freaking leak. Maybe the old geezer spilled coffee in his shed and doesn't remember."

"Coffee?" Antony wasn't buying it.

The mechanic threw up his hands. "You got a better answer?"

Antony looked at Ryan and he got the message.

This was a test. He walked by the man and stepped under the vehicle. Methodically, he scanned each part, looking for a possible leak. He loved how everything had its place, one piece fitting between another to work together to make the steel body move. From the undercarriage and the rust, he'd say the truck had to be at least fifteen years old.

He stepped out. "You got a dry rag?"

The mechanic grumbled before walking to a shelf on the wall of the garage and grabbing a rag. Antony stood there, his arms crossed.

When the mechanic came back, Ryan reached for the rag, but Antony grabbed his wrist. "You don't have any grease under your nails." The statement was made like an accusation.

Ryan held his cool by a thread and twisted his arm, breaking Antony's hold. What was wrong with this fucking town that everyone distrusted him? What the hell did he ever do to them, except leave with his mom when she moved away?

He stared Antony in the eyes. "They wouldn't let me work on a vehicle after I got shot until I was good enough to be discharged on my own two feet."

Antony had the grace to look away.

Ryan couldn't care less. He wasn't here to make friends. He just needed a temporary job and Antony needed some temporary help. That they'd gone to high school together obviously didn't count for squat.

Taking the rag, he wiped it along three seperate surfaces, using different areas of it to determine if there was anything coming out that he couldn't see. The three most common places came away dry. He frowned. Overseas, he'd found all manner of strange breaks because the beating the machinery was put through.

A hairline crack could be the beginning of a major failure. It was an old truck and from the dust and grime, he'd say the owner lived in the older section of town, farther out in the boonies. He checked two more spots and still nothing.

If the owner complained of a brown stain… an image of a tank part he'd requisition flashed through his mind, the metal still bearing the stain of human blood from its last life. He hated when he had flashes like that, but in this case, it gave him an idea.

He stepped out and lowered the truck.

Antony just watched him, but the mechanic leaned against a cabinet looking smug. "You couldn't find anything either." The statement pissed Ryan off, so he ignored it. If there was one thing the Army and Afghanistan had taught him, it was to hold his temper.

Popping the hood, he looked around the engine. Then he found what he'd suspected. Using the rag, he reached in between the fan and the radiator and pulled out a gray tail. "I found your leak." He held it up for Antony to see. "One of the gray squirrels must have crawled in while the truck wasn't running and when the owner turned it on…"

He shrugged. No need to go any further. He'd made his point. He walked over to a trash bin against the wall and dropped the tail in it along with the rag. When he came back, the mechanic was scowling at him.

Antony's lip quirked. "Let's go in my office."

# CHAPTER TWO

Lynzie pulled at the neck of her kelly-green turtleneck sweater as she waited while Ryan finished talking to the real estate agent about his grandpa's farm. She was so nervous, which was silly since they had been an item back in high school. It's not like they were strangers.

Then again, he'd changed so much. He'd filled out, grown muscles, even grown in height, and he smiled a lot more than she remembered. Every woman in the restaurant had noticed him when they walked in, but no one recognized him.

She felt a little justified in her shyness because she didn't know anything about his life over the last twelve years, so she didn't know how much the inner Ryan had changed. Hopefully, she'd find out now, though what good that information did her, she wasn't sure.

She couldn't help watching as he headed her way, his stride confident despite a slight hitch in his step, an apologetic smile on his lips.

He pulled out his chair. "Sorry. I hate doing that. It's just that the real estate agent who said we wouldn't get any bites until the new year, has already been contacted by a couple potential buyers. He was letting me know so I could take care of the worst issues first."

Now this was a subject she could sink her teeth into. "Are you selling it as a horse farm? It would be so great to have one again here." And she might be able to get a job doing what she'd been trained to do.

He looked askance at her. "Why? Did you want to go riding? The two horses Gramps has probably haven't been ridden in years, and they are pretty old, so I don't think it'd be a good idea."

"First, you'd want a vet to check them out, make sure there isn't severe arthritis. Do they get to run around the pasture at all on their own? If they haven't done much but walk and eat, we would need to start them on a light exercise routine before we did any riding. How old are they?"

Ryan's eyes widened. "Wait a minute. I've been around horses all my life, but wouldn't have known what to do with two who haven't been ridden in forever. How do you know so much?"

She felt her cheeks heat. "I earned a certificate as a horse trainer at the University. I was hoping to work with some racers or even one of the horse farms nearby, but it never panned out." She shrugged. "I waitress over at the Love Pub instead."

Ryan's dark eyes seemed to gleam with interest. "Horse trainer? If I remember correctly, you were a bit afraid of Gramps' horses."

"You're right. I was. But after watching you ride when I came over, I was determined to get over my fear. Now I love them. Unfortunately, except for your grandpa, Dianna and the Love's, no one has them anymore. Most of the farms have been sold and turned into developments." She grimaced. "Really nice developments."

He sat back. "I'm impressed."

"Don't be." She shrugged. "Though sometimes I use a horse training technique or two on my customers." She winked.

Ryan laughed, the tone far deeper than he had as a teen and so attractive her heart skipped. She may have always loved his dark eyes, but his smile now was breathtaking. He'd had his crooked teeth straightened and it lit up his whole face. He was different in so many ways, but he was still Ryan.

The waitress took that opportunity to interrupt them and take their order. Lynzie couldn't blame her for flirting with him, even though it irked her. He was the hottest new thing to hit Lucasville in a long time.

As soon as the waitress left, she resumed their conversation. "What about you? What have you been doing over the last twelve years? Are you married now? Children? Where are you living?"

Ryan shook his head. "No. No. And Florida."

She raised her eyebrows. "Come on. Spill."

He smiled again. "I've been too busy. I enlisted in the Army after high school. They discovered I was pretty good with cars and the next thing I knew I was working on tanks. By the way, in case you were wondering, cars and tanks are totally different beasts."

She grinned. "That sounds like the difference between a kitten and a tiger."

"Exactly. Unfortunately, there are a lot of Army tanks over in Afghanistan, so it wasn't long before they shipped me over there. I figured I wouldn't see much of the action, but I was dead wrong." His face turned serious for the first time since she'd seen him again and her gut tightened in response.

"Was it hard?"

He shrugged. "It wasn't easy. I only had a week left of my tour when I was shot."

"What? Where?"

"In my hip. They shipped me stateside after a brief stay in Germany. I went through a couple operations and a lot of therapy. But I had it easy compared to a number of my friends. Some didn't come home at all."

She couldn't resist the need to touch him any longer. She reached across the table and held his forearm. "I'm so sorry."

He looked at her hand as if it was a foreign object

he'd never seen, then his gaze met hers. "It taught me not to take things for granted and to make the most of my time here. That's why I looked you up."

His eyes, which were the darkest brown she'd ever seen on someone, appeared completely black. The intensity of his stare and the emotion coming off him had her hoping for things that couldn't be.

"Hey Lynzie. What are you doing here?" Andrew's voice was like a pitch fork scraping concrete.

She removed her hand from Ryan and forced herself to look at Andrew, who had just walked around the last table between her and him and bent over to give her a kiss.

She turned to Ryan, just as Andrew's lips connected. That he'd planned to kiss her on the lips not the cheek had to be obvious. "Ryan, this is Andrew Fielding. He's a transplant." She barely kept the derision out of her tone. "Andrew, this is Ryan. He's an old friend from my high school days."

Ryan stood, which caused Andrew to step back. Lynzie could tell her lover wasn't used to such nice manners. "Good to meet you." Ryan's voice was polite, but even though it had been twelve years, she could hear the reserve in it.

"Same here." Andrew shook hands then glanced at the front door. "Oh, I need to go. My lunch meeting has arrived." He placed his hand on her shoulder. "See you around."

She nodded. "Yup."

As Ryan took his seat, she could almost see his brain working, judging. She expected twenty questions. Why did Andrew have to show up at Laurent's when she was here. He was probably shocked to see her because the place was expensive.

"So what's the story with him? Boyfriend?"

She snapped her gaze to Ryan's. "Not exactly." She motioned with her head toward where Andrew had sat down with a woman in a navy-blue suit of excellent quality. The two of them were meeting all right, but if she had to put a label on what was happening in the booth in the corner, she'd call it foreplay.

Ryan looked toward the corner and his brow furrowed. "Ex-boyfriend."

She chuckled. "Not exactly that, either. We go out sometimes." And stay in sometimes. "As you can see, it is nothing serious."

"He's not good enough for you."

Her heart lurched at his words. She hadn't heard a sincere compliment like that in years, at least not from a man. "Thank you, but I think I'm the one who's not quite good enough, or should I say of the proper class."

Ryan studied her before he spoke and when he did, it was as if he chose his words carefully. "A man is more than his ability to provide financially. The value of man is based on character." He nodded toward the corner. "He lacks character."

Something in Ryan's tone had her believing he'd learned that in the Army. She shrugged. She didn't want to talk about Andrew. "How's your mom? Last time I saw her, her eyes were red from crying and she was packing boxes."

"That's right." He gave her a lopsided grin. "Luckily, she stopped crying soon after that and got angry instead. She divorced my dad. He couldn't seem to remember he was married when around other women."

"Oh, I thought it was just the one woman."

"No. I can't say my dad was as great as yours." He grimaced. "We moved in with my mother's parents who owned a horse farm in Florida. It's a beautiful spread. But when Mom remarried, my grandparents sold it. I was in the Army at the time, so I never had a chance to buy it."

Energy surged through her as she realized he must still love horses. Maybe she could work for him. "Were you thinking of buying Gramps' farm?"

In less than a second, he burst her dreams when he shook his head.

"No. I already bought one in Florida." He smirked. "There's no horses or staff there yet, but at least I own it."

She squashed her disappointment, something she did on a daily basis, and focused on him. "Are you going to breed horses? Or were you thinking of training them?"

"Neither."

She chuckled. "Are you just going to put them out to pasture?"

Ryan's eyes lit up. "Not that either. I'm going to start a Veteran's therapy program."

She'd never heard of such a thing. Then again, her dad was a policeman and was killed in the line of fire. No one she knew had served in the military and been overseas. "I'm not sure I understand. Does that mean you will use the farm like a summer camp, only with psychologists and physical therapists?"

"No, not exactly. It's more like a dude ranch. We will be using the horses for therapy and the quiet of the farm will help those with PTSD feel more comfortable. However, not every man or woman who comes back from combat has PTSD. There's about twenty percent who truly have it, but if you take into account the depression, guilt, anxiety, sleep disorders and readjustment to civilian life, there are a ton of ways my horses will be able to help."

She smiled, loving his enthusiasm. "Your horses? I thought you said you don't own any."

He nodded. "I don't, but that's where Gramps comes in. He offered me twenty-five percent of the final take on selling his farm if I'd help him sell it."

"Oh wow. That should be substantial, especially if you sell to a horse breeder or even a developer."

His smile was wide. "That's my hope. I would like

to start with five horses and a couple staff. Believe it or not I already have two friends who are helping just to have lodging. They are on disability pay and just want a safe, quiet place to hang their hat, so to speak. But while they both know their way around an M4, they don't have much horse experience."

Ryan's excitement was catchy. "Are your friends veterans too?"

"Yes, Jesse and Cooper. They are at the farm right now. I'd trust them with my life." He chuckled. "Actually, I had to a few times."

She couldn't imagine what it had been like for him. His upbeat excitement to help his fellow comrades was such a breath of fresh air. "How did you come up with this idea? Or was it that you wanted to help your friends using what you know?"

He shook his head. "I'd like to take credit for that, but I can't. I actually was told about a place that exists like this in Virginia and I went there myself. I admit, it wasn't for research." He lowered his voice and leaned forward, his smile gone. "I went because I needed help with my leg, but it was really an escape from having to fully readjust to civilian life again." He sat back. "I didn't have many expectations, but by time I was done, I knew what I wanted to do with my life savings."

Her heart swelled with pride in him at the same time she felt inferior. His sense of purpose, his caring, his life experience showed her exactly how small her own world had been.

Luckily, the waitress came by with their lunch and he started asking her about Lucasville. She was far more comfortable talking about a place she knew backwards and forwards.

By time they finished their meal, she was in complete awe of him.

After he paid, he walked with her outside. "I better get over to the garage. Antony wants me to do a couple hours work today. He still doesn't trust me. I never expected that."

She put her hand on his arm. "It's not his fault. All of us who have been here while Lucasville suddenly exploded have been burned a time or two. But to be fair, others have done very well like Renee Reese. Just give him a little time."

He looked at her. "What about you? Do you need time to trust me?"

She smiled. "No. You are still the boy I liked in high school, just better."

His grin was back. "That's good enough for me. So would you like to come over this weekend and give me a few pointers on Midnight and Toby?"

"I can come by Sunday. I don't work Sunday night."

"Perfect. You can stay for dinner."

What was she doing? "Sounds good."

"It will be. I'm cooking. You don't want to eat anything Gramps cooks. I found that out the hard way."

She rarely ran into Ryan's grandfather, but she'd heard he was forgetting things. "You know how to cook?"

He shrugged. "I've picked up a couple tips here and there. My specialty is smoked ribs. Do you like those?"

Oh, God could the man get any better? "I love smoked ribs."

"How about twelve hundred hours? I'd like your opinion on a few things, but I know you work late."

Her opinion? She ignored his use of military time. "Noon is fine."

He gazed into her eyes, a smile still on his face. "I'm really glad I came back here."

Before she could react to the thrill that buzzed through her chest, Ryan cupped her neck and kissed her.

The second his lips touched hers, her whole body came alive. At first the kiss was just a brush of a touch, but as he lifted away, he hesitated then came back and really kissed her, his tongue seeking entrance to her mouth, which she allowed.

As teenagers, they had been awkward at best in their kissing, but Ryan knew what he was about now as he commandeered her mouth with his tongue. She moaned as she kissed him back, loving his new taste.

"Excuse me."

At the sound of the strange voice, she pulled away and looked at the person who wanted to go into the restaurant. She didn't recognize the man, but still her cheeks heated.

"I'm sorry." Ryan spoke to the man then stepped away from the doorway, taking her with him, his hand at the small of her back, possessive.

Once they had walked a few steps away, he turned and faced her. "I know I should apologize for kissing you on the sidewalk in front of everyone, but I can't because I'm not sorry. I hope you're not offended."

She shook her head, not quite able to form words yet.

"Good." He looked at his watch. "I better get going. See you Sunday?"

She nodded.

He tipped his hat and strode off, the hitch in his step not quite as noticeable as it had been.

She watched him until he turned the corner, unable to take her eyes off him. Lifting her hand to her lips, she relived the kiss. Ryan Crawford had grown into the perfect man, just like the ugly duckling grew into a swan.

And he had opened her eyes to life's possibilities in just a few hours. If only—her doctor's appointment was Friday. Maybe she would get lucky and discover her home pregnancy test had screwed up.

"Old boyfriend?" Andrew's voice surprised her.

She turned to face him. His wavy blonde hair didn't move in the light breeze of the main street traffic. His light blue eyes laughed at her, as if to mock her wishes for a better life—like he had. She shrugged. "Not really. We were just in high school together." She looked around him. "All done with your meeting?"

He waved his hand dismissively, his expensive wool coat not even wrinkling with his gesture. "Just another of dad's clients. Are you working tonight?"

"Yes. Why?"

"I have a couple college buddies coming into town. Want to show them the Love Pub, remind them of our party days, when life was a breeze, instead of running to our fathers' beck and call." He grimaced.

Crap, the man had no clue what real work was. "I'll be there until close."

Andrew smiled. "Then I'll tell them we will have the best service by the prettiest waitress there."

"Laying it on a little thick, aren't you?" She raised her eyebrows.

He laughed. "Okay, you got me. See you tonight." Again, he lowered his head as if he would kiss her, and she stepped away.

"I have a few errands to run before work, so I'll see you later." She turned quickly and strode down the street, not daring to look back.

Andrew wasn't stupid. Even he'd sense there was

something different about her feelings toward him. Her only saving grace was she didn't think he had any feelings toward her, so she should be good.

# CHAPTER THREE

Ryan piled the spaghetti high on a plate and set it before his grandfather on the kitchen table. "I hope you're hungry."

His grandfather looked at it and sniffed. A small smile lifted his lips. "Looks like your mom taught you a thing or two."

"Yes, she did." He stifled the urge to say that she had to without his father around. "The sauce has beef and sausage in it."

His gramps twirled the pasta on his fork and blew on it. "Your grandma made one mean sauce, but after she died, I just used the jar stuff."

Ryan finished heaping food onto his own plate then sat down opposite Gramps. "I understand cooking for one. It doesn't seem worth the trouble." He twirled his own fork and blew on the pasta. It smelled almost as good as Lynzie did this afternoon, but it wouldn't even come close to tasting as good.

"Not bad." Gramps twirled another forkful of pasta.

He chewed on his mouthful and swallowed. "Did you order the hay today?"

"What hay?"

Ryan's gut tightened. "The hay to feed Midnight and Toby. We talked about it this morning. There's only enough left for a couple more days."

Gramps shook his head, a frown furrowing his brow. "You must have told someone else. I'll order it tomorrow."

Ryan opened his mouth to argue but it wouldn't change anything, so he kept quiet and twirled more pasta onto his fork.

"You had lunch with that girl today?"

Surprised, he stopped his movements. "You mean Lynzie Mullins? Yes, I did." Now how did Gramps know about that? He didn't tell him. Lucasville, for all it had grown, was obviously still a small town at heart.

"She's no good. She has no future. You can do better."

Denial leapt to his lips, but he forced down his anger. Gramps was old. He didn't know Lynzie. "Really? You liked her back when we were in high school."

Gramps frowned and his brow wrinkled in confusion. "I don't remember her. She ever come here?"

He relaxed. "Yes. She came here after school almost every day. Remember? She was the one who was afraid of the horses."

His grandpa's struggle to remember showed in his eyes before a look of panic came over him. "I don't know nothing about that. I do know that lady works in a pub. You can do better." He stuffed a forkful of pasta into his mouth, sauce coating his lips and one cheek.

Ryan watched, half of him sympathetic to the older man and half of him irritated. "Did you go to the hardware store today and order the lumber?"

"Sure did." Gramps grinned. "Harvey said it'll be delivered Friday. You'll have the barn looking good as new in no time."

"I'll get started on it Sunday. I have to work half a day at the Love garage Saturday."

Gramps scowled. "I don't see why you're working for Antony when you came here to work for me. Stupid people taking up your time. There's too much we have to fix here. Can't bring on more horses if those corral fences aren't mended."

Ryan's stomach tightened. Gramps was too confused and forgetful for it to be just old age. He would have to make a doctor's appointment for him. Getting him there would be tough, *if* Gramps remembered where they were headed. Maybe he wouldn't tell him until they were there. "We aren't getting any more horses. You want to sell Lazy Acres, remember? You said it was too much work."

His grandpa frowned again, but he looked

nervous. "I meant for the horses the new owners will bring."

Ryan nodded even as he took another mouthful. He chewed a long time, trying to get his stomach to relax and accept his food. It had become clear just in the few days he'd been at the farm that his grandpa needed as much care as the farm.

He couldn't count on his father to take care of that either.

It looked like he'd be in Lucasville right through the holidays. He'd hoped to be back on the Broken Oak. He'd call Jesse and see what her and Cooper's plans were. With no animals yet, he didn't have to worry about hiring someone to care for them, but he didn't like the idea of the place being empty.

Gramps stood, bringing his plate to the farmer's sink that was the showpiece of the large kitchen. "I'll wash the dishes. You go shower. You smell like grease."

He rose as well. "I do. Thanks." He placed his plate on the oak counter.

His grandpa waved him away. "I'll bring the horses in, but you better set your alarm because we have a lot to do tomorrow."

Ryan grinned. Times like now when his grandpa was his old self, he remembered how much he'd enjoyed the man back in his high school days. "Yes, sir."

"Bah." His grandpa started the water to fill the sink.

Ryan strode from the room. They'd have to buy a dishwasher if they wanted the place to sell. Maybe he could get Antony to give him some holiday hours. Some of the mechanics had families and might welcome a day off and he'd welcome the extra cash.

Lynzie waited impatiently for Coco to get off her shift. She'd ordered a hot fudge sundae while she waited, but her stomach was too tied up in knots to really eat it. Now all she had was melted vanilla ice cream soup with chocolate swirls.

Her own thoughts were starting to drive her crazy. Coco emerging from the back room was a relief.

"Okay, I'm free. What's up?" Coco started to sit.

Lynzie grabbed her arm and pulled her toward the door. "Not here."

"Boy, this sounds serious."

Lynzie gave her best friend a frown before exiting Shugs. She let go and started to walk down Main Street. "My appointment is tomorrow and I'm going crazy."

Coco gave her a sympathetic smile. "Ah, I understand. So what should we do for a distraction?"

Lynzie slowed her step, thankful that her friend knew her so well. "How would you feel about shopping for a New Year's Eve dress?"

Coco's eyes lit up. "Aren't you working New Year's Eve. You always work New Year's Eve."

Lynzie shook her head. "Not this year."

"How'd you manage that?" Coco grabbed her arm, bringing them to a stop in front of the local hardware store.

She grinned. "Lorenzo said he needed me for a Christmas Eve party. I told him fine, but he would have to give me New Year's Eve off."

Coco's eyes rounded. "Seriously?"

She nodded. "Yup. And he agreed."

"Wow. You have guts. I bet he was surprised."

She nodded and started walking again. "I think that's why he said yes. He was so surprised."

Coco laughed. "So where are we going to wear these new dresses we plan to buy?"

"Didn't you hear? There's a big New Year's Eve party for charity being held at Dianna's place." She hesitated. "I thought we could go even if we can't find dates."

Coco threw her hair over her shoulder, her streak of florescent pink hair catching the sunlight on the dry, cold day. "Speak for yourself. I'm a hundred percent positive I can find a date by then."

"Good." Lynzie stopped in front of the newest dress shop to hit Main Street. She'd been looking in the window for months, though now it was framed with white Christmas lights. She had no reason to go in until now, and if she would soon be fat with a baby, she wanted one last hurrah.

Of course, if she was pregnant, she couldn't drink. Everyone would know something was up. But what was the secret? They would know sooner or later. And it wasn't as if there were no other single mothers in Lucasville, though she could hear the whispers even now. There were certain people in town who would love to point their finger—

"So are we going in or are we just going to drool over these four black dresses in the window?" Coco cocked her head.

Lynzie shook her head to clear it. Another example of how she drove herself crazy with 'what ifs.' "Sorry. Let's go in. I don't want to wear black like every other woman in town. Let's find something that will make us stand out."

Coco's grin was contagious. "Oh good. I'm thinking maybe some gold lamé."

She opened the door. "Is that so your own soulmate will be able to find you?"

Coco stepped through, but stopped and waited for Lynzie to join her inside and the door to close. "I don't think my soulmate will be there. I'm pretty sure he's from another country, but I can still have fun."

It was her turn to widen her eyes. "You never told me that."

Coco shrugged. "To be honest, the idea just hit me a couple weeks ago, but the minute you mentioned my soulmate, I was suddenly sure it's true."

"Oh my God, that's awesome! Maybe he'll show up at the charity event."

Coco blushed. "That would be great, but what if I'm with a date."

Lynzie shrugged. "Then you dump him on the spot. You're the one who told me a person should never stand in the way of soulmates getting together."

"Can I help you?" A very pretty platinum blonde woman had approached. She was dressed in the finest clothes one could find in a size two. Next to Coco, she looked tiny.

Ready to defend her friend if needed, Lynzie stood straighter, gaining a couple inches over the woman in black pumps. "Yes. We are looking for a New Year's Eve gown."

The woman's smile barely held as if Lynzie couldn't possibly have a date for that holiday. The woman looked at Coco and her smile widened. "Coco, how good to see you again." She gave Coco a hug and her friend rolled her eyes.

When free of the embrace, Coco made introductions. "Lynzie Mullins, this is Patrice Reynolds."

After they shook hands, Patrice turned back to Coco. "You were right. Davey Russel was so wrong for me. I'm so glad we ran into each other. You did me a big favor. Now I need to return the favor. Let me see what we can find for you."

As Patrice led Coco toward a row of gowns, her friend looked over her shoulder.

Lynzie waved and smiled. She much preferred browsing without a store clerk looking over her shoulder. Walking past the black gowns, she found a clearance rack. The prices were still far beyond her reach, but she sifted through them anyway, just to make it look good.

She didn't even look at the dresses, just the price tags, getting more depressed as she went. She stopped at a tag that read ninety-nine dollars. It was more money than she'd ever paid for a dress, but she was here so she might as well look.

Parting the dresses, she swallowed. The gown was white, probably the reason it was such a low price compared to everything else. Pulling it out, she caught her breath. It was a retro halter neckline, with a band of gold applique around the waist.

Lynzie glanced over her shoulder to where Coco and Patrice were contemplating gowns. Quickly, she moved to the closest dressing room and stepped inside. Dropping her coat on the chair inside, she quickly stripped off her jeans, boots and sweater.

Reaching her hands under the plastic protector, she unbuttoned the neck and slipped the hanging ties over the hanger to pull the dress out. She held it up against her in front of the mirror. What she hadn't seen before was the gold sparkles in the white fabric that shimmered as she moved the dress. Unable to resist any longer, she quickly tried it on.

She stared at herself in the mirror. It was as if the dress had been made just for her. It made her medium sized breasts look bigger and her waist look very small. The extra material beneath the wide gold-lace waist, flowed as she moved, making her hips look more feminine.

The gold flecks accented her blonde streaks and the white made her skin look tanner than it was. She imagined Ryan seeing her in it and her heart stuttered. The image of his eyes darkening as he smiled at her was almost too real.

A knock sounded on the door, wresting her from her daydream. "Yes?"

"Lynzie, come on out. I need your help deciding." Coco sounded excited.

"Let me just change back into my clothes."

"You're wearing a gown?" Before she could say anything else, Coco opened the door. "Let me see."

She shook her head. "No. I just tried it on for fun."

Coco grabbed her wrist and brought her into the store, then stepped back. "Shoot Lynzie, you look gorgeous."

She could feel her cheeks heat as Coco's exclamation caught Patrice's attention. The woman walked over. "That does fit you perfectly, but if you're looking for a New Year's Eve dress, then it's all wrong. White is just not done."

"Of course. I just wanted to see what it looked like."

Patrice pursed her lips. "This isn't a costume shop." She turned to Coco. "Which will *you* try on?"

"I need Lynzie's opinion." Coco hooked arms with her. "Come over here and help me decide."

At Patrice's frown, she used her free hand to lift the bottom of the gown off the floor since she wasn't wearing shoes and went along with Coco. She felt like royalty in it. The gown hugged her body as the soft material whispered with her steps.

"Okay, I have it narrowed down to two. This red flouncy gown and the pink slinky one next to it."

Lynzie studied the two. Since the colors were Coco's favorites, she wasn't surprised, but what did seem odd was the style of the red gown. It looked like something from the 1950s with all the taffeta beneath the skirt. "Definitely, the hot pink. It even matches your hair."

Coco's look was wistful. "I know, it's amazing on the hanger, but the spaghetti straps…Patrice thinks the red because of the bolero jacket."

She swallowed a nasty retort. Coco had obviously told Patrice she didn't like to show her upper arms, but Lynzie didn't see anything wrong with her friend's arms. They were bigger than hers and less toned, but they were perfectly fine.

Her own were only toned because of all the pitchers of beer she had to lug at work. If she told Coco not to worry about the straps, her friend would ignore her. "I'd love to see you in the pink one."

"I'm afraid if I try it on, I'll love it."

She laughed. "That's not a bad thing. Get your butt in there this minute."

Coco hesitated for a second then finally lifted the hanger from its hook and walked into the dressing room. Patrice walked away, clearly unhappy with their choice, but luckily another customer came in to distract her.

Lynzie moved closer to the dressing room. She didn't want anyone to see her in the white and gold gown. There was a three-way mirror just outside the door, and she stood in front of it.

She studied herself thoroughly. Then she smoothed the gown over her abdomen. Could there really be a baby inside her? Half of her wanted it to be true and the other half was terrified.

The dressing room door opened. "I don't know." Coco's quiet voice was so unusual that Lynzie snapped her head around.

"What's not to know?" She guided her friend to stand in front of the mirror. "You look stunning."

Coco's eyes widened. "Shoot. I look sexy."

Lynzie smiled. "You bet you do. You look like Marilyn Monroe!"

Her friend's lips lifted in a hesitant smile as she

turned right then left to get a good view of herself. "I love it."

"Good. Then buy it."

Coco crossed her arms, covering her upper arms with her hands. "I'm not sure."

Lynzie wanted to slap Patrice and hug Coco, but she refrained from both and instead made Coco uncross her arms. "You are beautiful just the way you are. That gown was made for you. It's even the exact color of your pink streak of hair. I think it's fate."

Coco turned and looked at her, a mischievous gleam in her amber-colored eyes. "I'll buy this one if you buy that one."

She should have known that was coming. "You heard what Patrice said. White isn't the right color for New Year's."

Her friend cocked her head. "She also said I should wear the red gown."

Caught, Lynzie smiled. There was no way she'd allow Patrice to make Coco feel insecure about her curvaceous body. Not only did she rock the silky pink material with her hourglass curves, but it reflected how sweet she was inside. "Deal."

At Coco's excited laugh, she smiled. "I'll go change back into my jeans and meet you at the counter." She wiggled her eyebrows. "I can't wait to see the look on Patrice's face when we bring these up there. Think she'll give us a poor-taste discount?"

"I certainly hope so. I've never spent so much money on a piece of clothing." Coco grimaced. "Maybe we could keep it to two presents for each other this year?"

Lynzie nodded. "Sounds good to me. Now go change." As she walked back to the dressing room on the other side of the shop, she congratulated herself on helping Coco.

The two of them had been friends since high school, more specifically after Ryan moved away. She'd been so depressed, not realizing how much he meant to her until it was too late. If it hadn't been for Coco, she probably would have quit school all together.

As she slithered out of the white halter top gown, she couldn't help wondering what Ryan would think of it. Would he still be in Lucasville for New Year's? She definitely needed to find out on Sunday because she wanted him to be her date.

She stilled as she pulled her sweater over her head. If she was pregnant should she tell him? He was only in town until Lazy Acres sold, so why should it matter?

Her fingers touched her lips. Her women's institution told her it did.

# CHAPTER FOUR

---

Ryan finally guided Gramps out of the hardware store. "One more stop and we can get back to the farm."

His grandpa waved to a friend then gave him his attention. "I hope so. You still have the north fence to fix before the barn lumber is delivered tomorrow."

He grinned. Gramps was definitely making him work for his money, but he didn't mind. If he didn't need it so much for his own farm, he'd do all the work for free, but a rehabilitation farm without horses and staff wouldn't work.

"Where are we going?"

At his grandpa's question, he pointed. "Right here. Remember, you have a doctor's appointment."

Gramps frowned. "I do. No, I don't. I saw Doc Brady in December."

Ryan opened the door to the doctor's office, ushering his grandpa in. "That was a year ago."

"It was?" Gramps scowled as he scanned the

occupants of the waiting room. "Well, I don't need to go. I feel fine."

"Listen, if you walk out now, they'll charge you for the visit." His grandpa's rounded eyes made it clear what he thought about that. "Why don't you sit down and I'll get you checked in."

As Gramps made his way to a seat, grumbling under his breath, Ryan picked up a clipboard of papers from the receptionist. He sat down next to Gramps. "Do you want to fill these out, or do you want me to?"

Gramps waved his hand. "I've been coming here for years. I don't know why they need me to fill those out all over again. They don't even look at them. Doc Brady asks me the same questions every visit. I'm not wasting my time with that."

Ryan stifled his smile and filled out what he could. Everything else he wrote, *same as last year*. He doubted they got much more from his grandpa than that anyway.

He was halfway through when he heard a voice he recognized. Looking up, he grinned at the pretty picture Lynzie made leaning over the counter in a light green, long-sleeved sweater-dress, cowboy boots and straw cowboy hat.

"I can come any morning. I work nights."

The receptionist responded and Lynzie nodded. As she pulled on her dark blue coat, he couldn't let her go without talking to her. He'd fallen in love with her as a teen, but after seeing her again and learning she wasn't taken, his heart had skipped far ahead of him.

Not questioning his feelings, since he knew exactly how short life could be, he strode up to the counter. "Hey."

She turned, startled, her face pale and her green eyes round. "Ryan."

Suddenly, concern for her health flooded his psyche. "Are you okay?" He looked her over as if he could diagnose her.

"Yes, I'm fine. Just checking something out. No problem. What are you doing here?"

Relieved, he turned sideways and pointed to Gramps, who was busy chatting up the old lady sitting next to him. He lowered his voice, though his grandpa's hearing wasn't great to start with. "Gramps has been having some memory issues. I just want to get him tested."

Lynzie appeared to relax. "I'm so glad he has you here. I'd heard he wasn't doing that well. You're just what he needed."

And she was just what *he* needed. Now where did that come from? "He's okay most of the time. It's not like he'll forget who you are when you come by Sunday."

"Should I say hello now. I'd hate to embarrass him. I haven't seen him in a long time."

"That's a good idea." He took her hand and led

her over to his grandpa. "Gramps, look who's here. Lynzie Mullins. She's going to be visiting us Sunday."

He grandpa scowled. "I know you. You serve drinks at the pub."

She smiled. "That's right. I haven't seen you in a long time. How are you feeling?"

Gramps shook his head. "Didn't make nothin' of yourself did you. My grandson was in the Army, bought a horse farm and is helping me. What have you done?"

Lynzie's smile disappeared and Ryan's gut tightened. "Gramps. That's not nice. Lynzie has done a lot." He looked at her. "And she can tell us all about it on Sunday."

Before his grandpa could argue, he pulled her around and walked her outside. On the sidewalk, he let go of her hand. "I'm sorry about that. He's not all there as you can see. Just spouts off whatever he likes."

She placed her hand on his arm. "It's okay. He didn't say anything I haven't thought myself."

"Don't say that. Just because you haven't been able to land a horse training job, doesn't mean you haven't been successful. You're employed in an honest living and what's really great about you is your kind heart. A person's job doesn't determine who they are. Believe me, I know."

She gave him a crooked smile that told him he

hadn't convinced her. "Speaking of job, I need to go home and change for work. I much prefer jeans when serving beer. They're easier to wash."

"That makes sense." He looked into her green eyes, her insecurity about her own self-worth pulled at him. "You're still going to come Sunday, right? You won't let a grumpy old man scare you away, will you?"

She smiled a true smile and shook her head. "No. I'm too excited to see Lazy Acres again."

He gave her a sad face. "And here I was hoping you were excited to spend the day with me."

Lynzie winked. "That's the icing on the cake."

"I hope you have a sweet tooth." He loved the way her face revealed every thought.

She chuckled. "I really need to go. See you Sunday."

He wanted more than anything to grab her by the shoulders and kiss her, but he simply smiled and kept his arms at his sides as she walked away.

Damn, he was still in love with her. Was that why none of his relationships in the past lasted more than a few months? Had he been carrying a torch for Lynzie all these years?

He walked back into the doctor's office, feeling very lucky his Gramps had called him for help.

~

Lynzie picked up her phone to dial Andrew for

the third time in the last hour, but couldn't do it. "I need to tell him in person."

Coco, who sat on the couch in her living room, shook her head. "I don't think he deserves that courtesy."

She dropped her phone on the counter between her kitchen and living room and joined Coco on the couch. "You've never liked Andrew."

"Nope."

"Why not?" Part of her wanted to ask Coco if it was because Andrew wasn't her soulmate, but she kept her mouth shut.

"He's too self-involved. He's not a bad person in that he doesn't go out of his way to be an ass, but everything revolves around him. I can't imagine him making any sacrifice for a child, be it time or money."

She sighed. "That is the biggest concern I have. My dad spent every moment he could with me. It was as if he knew his life would end sooner rather than later."

Coco cocked her head. "He was a police officer. He knew he risked his life every time he went to work. He appreciated every second."

"Ryan said something similar. It's too bad we have to be in the line of fire to appreciate what we have." She looked down at her flat stomach.

"I'm only about four weeks according to Dr. Brady. It's hard to believe I'm going to be a mother.

Dr. Brady advised me to wait until my third month before telling anyone because that's when he can be more confidant that I will go full term. He's hesitant because it's my first pregnancy. It's hard not telling Mom and Paul…yet."

"Are you going to tell Ryan?"

Lynzie picked up one of her decorative couch pillows and held it against her chest. "I don't know. It's not like it affects him. He'll be leaving as soon as his grandfather's place sells."

"Seriously?" Her friend rolled her eyes. "That man is totally smitten with you."

Her heart leapt at Coco's words. "Why do you say that?"

"Because I have eyes. I saw how he looked at you when he came here and I watched you two outside Dr. Brady's office. I really thought he would kiss you."

"You spied on me?"

Coco laughed. "Now you sound as self-involved as Andrew. No, I actually found a parking space on Main Street for a change and was waiting to cross the street to go to work when you two stepped outside."

"It doesn't really matter. I'm pregnant with Andrew's baby. I doubt that Ryan would be interested in anything long term with me."

"But you don't know that. I think you should tell him and let him decide."

Lynzie shook her head. "Whoa, slow down. You

don't want me to tell Andrew about his own baby face to face, but you want me to tell Ryan?"

Coco shrugged as she stood. "I can't help it if I like one better than the other, and I think you do too."

Did she? Crap, she did. Her heart was totally taken with Ryan. "Okay, I'll tell him tomorrow." She held up her hand. "But I'm not getting my hopes up for anything lasting. He's leaving when Lazy Acres sells and yes, he *will* leave. He has a horse farm of his own in Florida."

"Florida?" Coco squinched up her nose. "Seems like a silly place to have horses."

She shrugged. "That's what he said."

Coco shook her head as she put on her jacket. "I have to run. My closer for the ice cream shop called in sick, so I have to lock up. Are you working tonight?"

Lynzie nodded. "It's not like I can call in sick for being pregnant."

Her friend laughed. "Nope. At least not yet." Coco leaned down and gave her a hug then let herself out of the apartment.

Lynzie glanced at the clock. She needed to get ready for work, but she didn't feel much like moving. The temperatures outside were probably already falling and the Christmas tree she and Coco had bought stood in the corner waiting for her to add the lights and ornaments. The temptation to call in sick was strong, but then her stomach growled.

She looked down. Wow, she was eating for two now. She stood then walked into her kitchen. She had a frozen meal in the freezer, so she took it out and microwaved it. While she waited, her hunger grew exponentially and she started to feel queasy.

At the ding of the microwave, she pulled out her food and blew on it to cool it. Beyond hungry, she took a bite and burned her tongue. "Damn." She grabbed up the meal and stuck it in the freezer. After counting to thirty, she pulled it out and started to eat.

If this was what being pregnant was all about, she needed to go grocery shopping.

Ryan led Midnight out into the north pasture, a place the horse probably hadn't seen in more than a year. The newly fixed fence with its quick paint job made that pasture available to the horses again.

He released the black Quarter horse and turned back toward the barn, his eyes straying toward the dirt driveway. It wasn't even close to noon, but he was excited to see Lynzie. He had some news to share with her.

The bells of the south church rang, letting everyone know that mass had ended. He loved the sound as it reminded him of some of his past fun days when he and Lynzie would leave church and go on a picnic down by the crick or pooled their money to get themselves a banana split at Shugs. When the bells stopped chiming, he went inside the barn again.

After releasing Toby into the north pasture to join his sister, he went back to the barn and the section behind the stalls that needed the boards replaced. Without hesitation, he lifted the crowbar and started the process of removing them from the barn wall.

A couple of the boards broke into pieces, their rot was so thorough. The work was hard, but it felt good to be productive again. Once he'd finished removing the old boards, he grabbed up the water bottle he had sitting on a haybale and drank. Next he needed to cut the boards.

The hardware store had delivered the lumber right to the barn and luckily it had been sunny the last couple days, but they were calling for rain on Monday, so he needed to get this project done as soon as possible.

As he stepped outside, he squinted against the sun to look at the driveway again. There was no car in sight, not even the dust cloud from one. Lifting the boards he needed, he lugged them back into the barn and put one across two sawhorses. In no time, he'd measured and cut them all.

Unable to help himself, he picked up his water bottle and as he drank, he strode outside once again to look for Lynzie. He cupped his hand over his eyes and looked up at the sky. It had to be close to noon by now.

Without an excuse to be in the yard, he went back into the barn and moved the first board into place. It was really a two-man job, but his Gramps was in town again. He loved hanging out with Harvey, and since the hardware store was closed on Sundays and he'd have the owner's undivided attention, he didn't expect his grandpa back until dinner time.

Holding the board and nailing in the nails tested the limits of his strength, but he managed. Having worked up a sweat, he stripped off his t-shirt and grabbed the next board. It was slightly easier with the first one in place.

Each one overlapped the other, making for a tight fit. When he was done, he stepped back. "Now that looks good."

Picking up another water bottle, he left the barn to look at the outside of the repair. He studied the light brown wood against the weathered boards that surrounded it and groaned. After fixing the barn, he would have to paint the whole thing. Tilting the water bottle over his head, he let it cool him off.

Too bad he couldn't use the same tactic to paint the barn, but he doubted there were any large vats of paint that attached to a crane in Lucasville.

"Ryan?"

# CHAPTER FIVE

---

Ryan spun at the sound of Lynzie's voice. She stood there in a pair of blue jeans, a buttoned-down collared shirt, cowboy boots, her straw hat and a coat thrown over her arm. "I didn't hear you arrive."

When she didn't respond, he stepped closer. "Lynzie?"

"Is that where you were shot?" She stared at the scar next to his collar bone in confusion.

He laughed. "No, not here." He pointed to the scar. "That was from a fall out of the hayloft of my mother's parents' barn. Just me being a stupid teenager."

Her green gaze finally met his. "But you *were* shot."

He nodded, sobering as he thought of that moment overseas when the bullet connected with his body. Who would have thought it could be that painful. "I was. Caught one in the hip. Thought I would lose the leg, but I had a miracle worker for a surgeon. That's why I did the horse therapy."

"I'm so sorry." Her gaze was so caring, he had to touch her.

Cupping her face, he stroked her cheek with his thumb. "Thank you. I got off easy."

She reached her hand up and pushed back his wet hair. "I hate the thought of you getting hurt. Will you be going back?"

He shook his head. "No. Honorably discharged."

"I'm glad." The two words left her lips in pure relief, even as her hand came down to rest on his shoulder.

He didn't even try to resist. Tilting her head up, he lowered his lips to hers. She was everything soft and sweet. Her lilac scent filled his nostrils, reminding him of their days together as teens.

But they weren't teens anymore and as his tongue moved into her mouth, he was thankful they were two grown adults. He pulled her against him, craving the soft curves he felt give way to his hard body.

He broke the kiss and moved his lips to her neck. She tasted so good, far better than he remembered. He wanted her.

Lifting his head from her skin, he stared at her until she opened her eyes. "Lynzie." His throat closed over the words he wanted to utter. *I love you. I want you.*

"I missed you so much." Lynzie looked away. "I almost ran away from home twice, but Mama was alone and I just couldn't do it."

Guilt for not coming back sooner crept into his heart. "I should have returned earlier, but first it was the Army and then the rehab and with my father's and my relationship…" The fact was, if he had really loved her then, he would have come back.

She gave him a shy smile. "We were just too young. How could we be sure what we felt would last. Even now, I wonder if these feelings I have for you are real or just curiosity about what could have been."

He gave her a crooked smile. "About what could have been? I wonder about what could be."

She pulled out of his arms. "Is Gramps here? I should probably say hello. I don't want to be rude, despite what he thinks of me."

Ryan rubbed the back of his neck, bothered by her withdrawal. "Honest Lynz, I have no idea where he got all that. When we were young, he liked you."

She shrugged. "Like I said. It's okay. You said you wanted my opinion." She pointed to the newly repaired barn wall. "If it's about your fix, I can't say I have a lot of experience, but it looks good to me."

"Thank you, but that's not why I asked you here. Let me grab my shirt and I'll show you what I'd like your opinion about." He strode into the barn and pulled his shirt over his head. If he really wanted Lynzie, he needed to slow down.

But everything in him urged him to tell her how he felt and make love to her. Life was too short. If she felt anything for him, which he was pretty sure she did, then he wanted to pursue it to the end.

Walking outside, he found her leaning against the fence to the north pasture. His heart jumped at the sight. She looked so natural here on the farm. The glimmer of an idea started in the back of his head. She was a horse trainer after all.

He stepped up next to her and leaned his elbows on the fence. "Does the place look like you remember?"

She nodded. "It does, for the most part. Obviously, the new wood on the barn is different." She gave him a smirk. "And the house is showing some of its age, but the property looks the same."

"I've been working every day, around my schedule at the garage, to get it fixed up as quickly as possible. We actually have someone coming right after Christmas to look at it. My realtor says the man is from Scotland and has a lot of money."

Lynzie stepped back from the fence. "That's great."

Her words sounded positive but her face said it was terrible. "You don't sound as excited as I'd hoped."

"I'm sorry. I *am* happy that you may have a buyer. It's just that, you just got here. I admit to hoping that you would stay for a little longer than a couple weeks."

"Actually, that makes me feel a lot better. I'm not in as much of a hurry to leave as I was when I first decided to come here. I'm sure it will take weeks for the negotiations, the closing, and the move out date."

She nodded, clearly not convinced. "What about Gramps? Where is he going?"

"Actually, that's another thing I wanted your opinion about."

"Me?"

He nodded. "Yes. You are one of the few people who know the real story behind my mother's divorce." Finding out his father had a mistress and two children by her on the side had hit him hard, especially when he realized that was why his father never spent any time with him.

She nodded. "I do and I've never told anyone. Not even Coco."

"I appreciate that." He looked out over the land and at the two horses at the other end of the pasture. "I realized when I returned here that I had ignored Gramps as much as my father did and that wasn't right. Gramps had always been good to me. He tried to fill in for my father."

She smiled. "I remember him coming to all your basketball games."

"He did." Ryan grinned. "He should get a medal for that. I was no Kieran Love, but I did have fun and Gramps supported me one hundred percent. I should have returned sooner, but now that I'm here, I think I need to take more interest in what Gramps will do. He says he'll move into a condo over in the newly developed area of Lucasville. He likes the idea of having a pool outside that he doesn't have to take care of."

"I sense a 'but' coming."

"Yeah. He's been forgetting a lot of things and I've watched him get confused. That's why I took him to see Dr. Brady. They ran some tests and we'll have the results next week."

She listened intently. She really did care about his grandpa. "So what are you thinking?"

He took a deep breath. "I'm thinking of taking him with me to the Broken Oak."

"That sounds like a good plan, but I can tell your hesitant. Why?"

He rubbed the back of his neck. "If he does have Alzheimer's like I suspect, I'm not exactly trained to care for someone with that. I can rebuild an engine, but caring for someone with such a devastating disease is beyond me."

She nodded. "But you also can't leave him on his own and I'm betting you're wondering if you should set him up in a care facility. Right?"

"Yeah, but I'd hate to do that now. He's not that bad yet and I hear the drugs they have can really slow down the process. On the other hand, what if he forgets to take his medicine? I can't keep an eye on him here if I'm in Florida."

She tipped her hat back. "I suppose I could look in on him for you. Maybe once a day, but you may have to hire a professional eventually."

He didn't speak, his words stuck in his throat at her generous offer. He swallowed hard then pushed his words out. "I couldn't ask you to do that. I'm just looking for your opinion on what I should do."

"Don't be silly. I work evenings and nights, so I could stop by around lunch time…that is if he'll let me. He didn't seem so keen on me the other day at the doctor's office."

Embarrassed by Gramps' behavior, he brushed it off. "I have no idea where he got those ideas about you. I'm guessing he's mixing you up with someone else."

Lynzie obviously didn't believe him. "It would only be a temporary solution though. If it would make you feel better, you could pay me." She smirked, her eyes lighting with mischief.

She may think it silly, but he could never ask her to look after his grandpa without paying her. Plus, it could give him an excuse to come back to Kentucky on a regular basis and see her. Even at the thought of seeing her only once a month, his heart slowed.

He was hopeless. In town a mere week and he'd already become addicted to Lynzie all over again, and this time with a man's heart, not a boy's. He nodded. "I like that Gramps would know you. Let's keep that as a possibility."

She smiled. "And I'll see if I can't charm him out of his low opinion of me."

He pulled her into his arms. "You must be an amazing charmer because I think so highly of you, I have you on a pedestal way above me."

She frowned and looked away. "You're just seeing what you want to see. I'm—"

He didn't want to hear her put herself down one more time, so he kissed her. This time, he let her know exactly how he felt about her. As his tongue tangled with hers and he pulled her tight against him, he hoped she understood.

Lynzie silently sighed as Ryan's mouth met hers. Wrapping her arms around his neck, she let him take her away to a make believe world where they were together forever. The scent of hay, one of her favorite smells, clung to him from his work in the barn. His muscular arms wrapped around her as if he never wanted to let go and his kiss was a mix of passion and tenderness.

It was that sweetness that finally helped her to pull away before she started to cry for what could have been.

"Lynzie." His whisper was that of someone in love and though her heart jumped for joy, her mind at least was still functioning. She put her finger across his lips and shook her head. "Aren't you supposed to be getting my opinion on something else?" She gave him half a smile, the best she could muster at the moment.

He blinked as if he'd forgotten where they were and what they were doing. His hold on her loosened and she broke away, but hooked her arm around his, hoping for a lighter feel to their day. "You do remember what that was, don't you?"

He smiled sheepishly. "Guess I got a little off track."

She shrugged. "It happens. So what else do you need my input on? I have to say I'm feeling quite helpful."

"Good, because I need all the help I can get." He said it with a smile, but she could hear the truth behind his words.

He had a lot of plans for the near future and was obviously not one hundred percent sure he could pull it off. But she knew he could.

He pulled his arm from hers and jumped over the pasture fence. "I'd like your expert opinion on Midnight and Toby."

Ah, so that's why he let go of her. She nodded and stepped up on the bottom rail. Swinging one leg over then the other, she jumped down on the other side. When she turned, she caught him looking at her butt. When his gaze met hers, he wiggled his brows. "You sure have grown up."

She swatted him on his arm. "You have no room to talk. Look at you. You grew up and out. No wonder no one in town recognized you at first."

He sniffed as if hurt. "Not even you."

Linking her arm in his again, she smiled up at him. "I would have, given time. I always had a thing for your eyes."

"My eyes?" He laughed. "And here I thought it was my charming personality."

"Well, there was that, too. But now there is a whole lot more." She winked, pleased to have their conversation at a much more surface level of flirting.

She was able to keep them at that level as she looked over the two old horses, concluding that no matter who bought the farm, Ryan should take the horses with him to be fair to them. Even if the new owner wanted a horse farm, he would give his own horses preference and neither Midnight nor Toby would sweeten a deal on the property. They were good horses, but they were old and deserved to live out the rest of their lives being pampered.

Then he'd brought her inside, asking her opinion on everything from the position of the furniture to curtains. The house wasn't in bad shape, but there were water stains on a couple ceilings from before he'd fixed the roof, and he still needed to replace the front steps or someone would surely go through the rotten wood. She sincerely hoped he found a buyer that would give Gramps his asking price.

While Ryan cooked his ribs outside in the smoker, she set the table. She glanced at the clock concerned that it was getting dark and Gramps still hadn't returned. He was in his seventies and still drove, which if Lucasville hadn't grown so much since she was a teen, wouldn't have worried her. But the traffic was crazy these days, and the roads weren't wide enough to accommodate the fast growth.

Even on Main Street where Gramps had gone, people were forever running red lights and going way over the speed limit. She was probably a little late to be worrying about him. After all, in the last twelve years since Ryan had left, she hadn't worried too much about his grandfather.

Then again, she'd done exactly what Ryan had, made Gramps guilty of his son's transgressions. Now that she understood her mistake and Ryan's concern for Gramps, she couldn't help being nervous about him. Her offer to look after him had been genuine, but if Ryan wanted to pay her, she wouldn't turn it down. She would need every cent she could earn for her and her baby.

There was still no change in her body shape, though she had already started to dread her mornings, and even when she got hungry and didn't eat right away, she started to turn green. She would tell her mom at Christmas even if it was barely four weeks. Her mom would have a lot of good advice and she wanted to hear all of it.

Which meant she had to tell Andrew before

then. Christmas was Thursday. She wasn't sure why she'd avoided telling him. Maybe it was Coco's initial reaction, or maybe it was her own inner fear that Andrew wouldn't help her.

Headlights caught her attention, and she breathed a sigh of relief. It had to be Gramps. Moving to the cabinet, she pulled out glasses for all of them. Ryan was having iced tea and she would have water. When the door opened she turned. "Hi, Gramps."

He stopped. "What are you doing here?"

# CHAPTER SIX

Lynzie smiled kindly. "It's Sunday. Remember, I came over to help Ryan with a few items around the farm? He's cooking his smoked ribs for dinner. What would you like to drink?"

Gramps looked confused then he sneered. "Don't think you're going to get any of my money through Ryan. I won't let him have a cent if he hooks up with you."

Stunned, she leaned back against the kitchen sink. "I don't want any money and I'm not 'hooking up' with Ryan. We're just old friends."

Gramps snorted. "That's not what I'm hearing. You want to rise above your social status by getting your claws into my grandson. Let me tell you, Missy. I'm not letting that happen."

Social status? What social status? That wasn't Gramps talking. It appeared she needed to have a talk with Harvey. She smiled kindly. "Gramps, I'm not after anything. I'm perfectly happy with my life just the way it is. Now what can I pour you to drink?"

He mumbled something under his breath that she couldn't hear.

"What?"

"I said I'm not eating with the likes of you." He turned around and headed down the hallway. As he stomped upstairs, Ryan came in.

"Where's Gramps? I saw his car pull in."

She grimaced. "He went upstairs. I'm afraid he won't eat if I'm here. I better go."

"What? No. I'll go up and drag his rude ass back down here. Excuse my language." Ryan's anger glittered in his eyes and his hold on the rib platter could break it at any minute.

She took the platter from him and set it on the table. "No, don't make him do that. I think someone has been feeding him a bunch of bull. I'll talk to Harvey and see if I can't get to the bottom of it."

Ryan grabbed her wrist. "I don't care who he's been listening to, the old man has been living alone for too long and has forgotten his manners. It will do him good to go to bed without dinner. You, on the other hand, need to sit down."

She hated that she was a source of conflict for the two men, but one look into Ryan's eyes and she understood he meant business. "Okay. I'll eat, but then I need to go home. I have to finish decorating my apartment." Not that anyone but she and Coco would see it.

Ryan pulled out a chair at the table. "Good. I worked hard on these ribs." His smile relaxed her, and she gave him one in return.

He made a production of loading her plate with ribs and corn on the cob until she finally put her hands over her plate to keep him from piling more food on it. "Whoa, I'm not as big as you. Maybe you should take this one."

"You're right. I'm used to Cooper and Jessie. They eat more like I do. Whatever you can't finish, just take home for lunch tomorrow."

She bit into a rib and groaned with pleasure.

"Is that good or bad?" Ryan raised his brows with his hesitant question.

She nodded, "Hmm, hmm." She didn't want to take a second away from enjoying the smoky, sweet and tangy flavor all in one bite.

He grinned. "Glad I haven't lost my touch."

She shook her head, but continued to gnaw every piece of meat off the bone that didn't fall off. When she finally took a breather and wiped her hands on the paper towels she'd piled on the table, she found him staring at her with a strange look on his face.

Thanks to his very dark brown eyes, it was hard to tell what he thought. "You're looking thoughtful."

"I guess I am. It's all this." He gestured toward the entire room. "Coming back here, seeing you, the holidays around the corner."

"I can't imagine what it would be like. I've never left Lucasville."

He paused, his iced tea half way to his lips. "Why not?"

She tore her gaze from his muscular forearm and shrugged. "After I couldn't find an apprenticeship within driving distance, I did look farther away, but I never applied. I just couldn't see leaving my mom alone."

He finished swallowing and placed the glass back down. "How is your mom?"

She smiled. "She's great. She fell in love again, to a man who didn't have a risky job. His name is Paul Hubbard. I'm not sure if you remember him. He used to own Hubbard Insurance, but he passed it down to his son."

"I vaguely remember the sign. How long has she been married?"

She had to think about that. "Over three years now. I'm just thrilled she's so happy. Coco did some of her matchmaking magic with that one."

Ryan lowered his corn. "Matchmaking. Didn't people think she had some kind of voodoo power or something?"

"Or something. She really does have it." Lynzie took a sip of water and wiped her mouth. "It's weird. She says she can see when two people are soulmates. She doesn't tell them unless they ask, but she and I try to get soulmates to meet if they haven't yet."

Lynzie sighed. "Unfortunately, some of the newer residents of Lucasville have discovered Coco's ability and bother her a lot. She says she doesn't mind because they usually come to Shugs with their 'date' and she makes them buy ice cream before she'll tell them if they're soulmates. Actually, it's the women who ask."

Ryan wiped his mouth and dropped his paper towel on his empty plate. "Has she found your soulmate yet?"

"I don't know. I refuse to ask her. Though I do like helping her play matchmaker when we have time." She smiled at the memory of the fun times they had. "My mom and Paul are just one example. There are over twenty five happy couples in town that are soulmates that Coco discovered and helped along."

He gave her a doubtful look. "Hmm, I wonder if it has anything to do with her name."

"What? What does that have to do with it?"

He shrugged. "You have to admit it's unusual. So an unusual name for an unusual ability."

"Really? Coco's mom named her after Coco Channel the designer. I would think for that theory to work, Coco would have a knack for sewing but she can't even sew a button on straight." She shook her head at him, her lips quirking up a bit at his silliness.

Ryan's look turned mysterious. "Now your name is not only beautiful but unique, like you."

Oh no. That look and his words were causing

her food to do somersaults in her belly. "I'm just like everyone else. Mom just wanted a different spelling."

He sat there shaking his head, his look intense in his silence. It was that full-on *let's get together forever* look that scared her.

She scraped back her chair. "I should probably head home now. I want to get the rest of those decorations up. Besides, I'm sure Gramps is starving by now." She stood, quickly.

Ryan shot to his feet. "Wait. Let me wrap this up for you." He took her still half-full plate to the counter.

"I'll wait outside." Before he could stop her, she grabbed up her coat and walked out the side door and into the yard. She started to pace to keep warm. She needed to remember Ryan would be leaving soon. The Scottish buyer was due in tomorrow afternoon. He could very well make an offer and Ryan be gone by New Year's Day.

She stopped. She had planned to ask him to the charity dance, but now she wasn't sure. She didn't want him to think that anything could happen between them. After all, she was pregnant with Andrew's baby.

"Here you are." Ryan came out the side door and strode toward her. Even in the dark with the warm light from inside barely lighting the yard, he was impressive. There was a confidence despite the slight hitch in his step and his body exuded strength while his white smile revealed his warm heart.

He handed her the bag that felt far heavier than what was on her plate. "Lynzie, I hope I didn't work you too hard today."

She smiled. "Not at all. You did all the hard work." And she'd dream about his wet chest tonight just as she'd seen him when she first walked up to the barn.

He took her hand. "When can I see you again? I have to work at the garage in the morning and the buyer is coming in the afternoon."

She shook her head. "And I work at the pub until two in the morning. Plus with the holidays, things are just very busy."

"Lynz, why are you brushing me off? You don't kiss someone like you kissed me today and then disappear."

She tried to pull her hand from his grasp, but he wouldn't let go. "I shouldn't have come today, but I missed you. I just wanted to catch up a bit more."

He shook his head. "I'm not buying it. What is it? Is it that guy who came by when we were at lunch the other day?"

She snorted a laugh, then covered her mouth with her free hand, completely embarrassed.

He ignored her unladylike snort. "Tell me."

She might as well tell him and get this torture over with. "I'm pregnant."

He looked at her confused as if he didn't understand what that meant, but then he finally let her hand go. "You *do* have someone special in your life."

She shook her head. "Only the baby." She laughed a little hysterically as her heart began to break all over again. "I don't even know if it's a boy or a girl yet."

"I don't understand."

Neither did she. She didn't understand why she had to find him again when it was too late. She didn't understand how she could feel so strongly about him in so short a time after determinedly putting him out of her mind.

Her eyes began to water and she didn't care. "You know, I don't either." Turning away, she stalked to her car. Half of her wanting him to come after her and the other half hoping he wouldn't. She opened the door and sat inside, automatically putting the food on the passenger seat and starting the vehicle.

When she turned the headlights on, he still stood where she'd left him. His face a study in confusion and hurt. She should have never come. She should have never encouraged him. They couldn't have forever and he deserved one.

Turning the steering wheel, she made a U-turn and drove down his driveway. Tears began to fall but she ignored them, the pain in her heart taking all her focus.

By time she pulled into a parking space behind her building, her tears had dried. She wasn't living in happily ever after land. She lived in the real world and she needed to stay there even if her teenage hero had come back to town a real hero.

That wasn't her life. Her life was with the baby she carried, and it was time she told the dad so he could face the reality of his actions as well.

Opening the door to her apartment, she switched on the lights and brought the food into her kitchen. She was about to throw it away when her practical side took over.

She was eating for two now. No need to waste good food in her real world. She put the leftovers in the refrigerator then went into her room to change into her comfy sweats.

Then she walked into her living room and picked up her phone. Sitting on her couch, she dialed. "Hi, Andrew. I have something important to tell you."

Lynzie looked at the clock. Five more minutes and the Christmas Eve party would be over. Thank God. She was beyond exhausted. Waking up every morning sick as a dog had her taking a nap every afternoon before work, but she just never felt rested.

Of course, Andrew wasn't helping. He kept texting her. Everything from "Are you sure it's mine?" to "You need to get a paternity test." to "Let's get together and discuss arrangements." And those were the nice ones.

She did feel for him. When she'd first found out she wasn't sure what to think. She still wasn't sure, but she'd become used to being unsure. In between vomiting and napping, she started to look at her one bedroom apartment and thought about different ways she could arrange it for the baby.

It would work for a little while, but she'd need a bigger place eventually. Her mom would insist on her moving in, and she wasn't sure she could resist. It could help, but she felt as if that was taking the easy way out. It was bad enough she would have to ask her mom to babysit because she couldn't afford a sitter.

And then there was the one person she hadn't seen in three days…Ryan. Every time she thought of him, the image of him standing there in his dark yard looking confused and hurt filled her head.

"Hey Lynzie, lock the front door." Lorenzo walked in from the back office. "We don't need any partiers coming back for more."

"Got it." She dropped the towel she'd been wiping down the tables with and strode to the front door. As she reached it, she hesitated, her heart palpitating in her chest. Outside the glass door, standing in the freezing cold, was Ryan in his white cowboy hat and a black leather jacket.

Pulling herself together, she opened the door, the frigid Christmas Eve air blowing against the light dress she'd worn to work for the private party. "Ryan, what are you doing here?"

He stopped his pacing and moved toward her. "I came to walk you home."

"Well, get inside. You're going to freeze to death." She opened the door farther then locked it behind him. She had no idea how Lorenzo would feel about this, but she wasn't going to let Ryan freeze. Besides, her curiosity was far too strong to tell him to go home, and her heart was far too excited to see him. "It will still be another half hour or so. We just started cleaning up."

"No, it won't." Lorenzo strode toward her with her coat. "Get out of here. It's Christmas Eve. I'll have Stella finish the clean up after Christmas."

"Really?" She stared at Lorenzo in shock.

He smiled, holding her coat out to her. "Yeah. I'm getting soft in my old age. I saw how you were dragging your butt around here tonight. Go. Have a couple days of rest and be back here the day after Christmas."

She smiled. "Thanks."

He waved her off and walked away. She stared for a minute, still trying to grasp the fact that she wouldn't have to clean up the mess the party goers had left.

"Here, allow me." Ryan pulled her coat from her hands and held it out for her.

As she put her arms in each sleeve, she tried to remember the last time a man had done that for her, but the only memory that came to her was the Harvest Moon dance in high school when Ryan did the very same thing.

She buttoned up her wool coat and pulled her mittens from her pockets. "We have to go out the back."

"Lead the way."

She led him through the kitchen and out the back door. They started down the alley toward Main Street.

"You walk through this every night you work?" His gruff tone made it clear he didn't like it.

"I do and I have for seven years now and not once have I run into trouble." She bumped into him on purpose. "Unless you're going to cause me trouble."

He didn't take the bait, instead he kept silent.

Too thrilled that he'd come by, she looped her arm around his since he'd stuffed his bare hands in his pockets. He didn't say anything or pull away, so she figured it was okay.

They continued toward her apartment which was only a couple blocks away, but he still didn't say anything.

The bells from the south church started to ring, and he stopped walking.

She clarified in case he'd forgotten. "They're calling people to midnight mass."

He finally looked at her. "I remember them. My mom used to insist that we go. You weren't there."

She shook her head. "Not after dad died. Mom held a lot of resentment in her heart. She loved him so much."

They continued walking, the bells chiming beautiful, joyful music through the cold night air. When they got to the door of her apartment, she took off her mitten to get the key into the lock, but it fell from her hand and onto the landing.

Before she could bend over, Ryan had recovered it and unlocked her door. He opened it, letting her precede him inside.

She flicked the switch and her Christmas tree lit up. She loved having just the Christmas tree lights on.

Ryan closed the door behind him as she unbuttoned her coat and hung it on a peg near the door. "You can take off your coat. If you like, I can serve you up a piece of pecan pie. I made one to bring to Mom's for Christmas, but I made a second one just for me."

"No, thank you." He took off his hat and hung his coat next to hers. Beneath it he wore a green flannel shirt and a pair of black jeans. And of course, he also wore cowboy boots.

She headed to her kitchen. "I can warm up some cider if you like. I'm afraid I have no alcohol." As soon as she said the words, she wished she hadn't. It just reminded them both about her condition. "Or I have cold cider, coffee and sweet tea."

Ryan stood looking at her tree as if it held the answer to all the questions in his head. "I'm good."

She poured herself some cider, just for something to do. Unlike Coco, she didn't need to be talking all the time. Then she moved to the couch, dropping her hat on the end table, and sat. The lights reflecting off Ryan's tan face, were soothing as she took a sip of cider.

He finally turned toward her and put his hat on the coffee table. "I needed to see you."

Her heart leapt at his words. "I'm glad. I felt bad about the way I left on Sunday."

He walked to the couch and sat next to her. "You surprised me."

"I know. I'm sorry. It was quite a surprise to me as well."

He rubbed the back of his neck. "Who is the father?"

When she first started seeing Andrew, she'd been proud of the fact, but when put next to Ryan, he paled in comparison. In fact, she was embarrassed to admit she'd slept with him. But this was the real world, as she kept telling herself, and the last thing she'd do is lie about such an important detail. "Andrew Fielding, the man that stopped by our lunch table last week."

Ryan seemed to relax, but that had to be her imagination. "And is he happy about the prospect of being a father?"

She squirmed. "Wow, you get right to the heart of the matter don't you?"

"I do when it's important."

She gazed into his dark eyes and knew she couldn't lie. "Not really. He keeps asking for a paternity test and in the next message tells me we can make an arrangement. I get the feeling he's talking about a financial arrangement."

Ryan nodded as if it was as he expected. "He's too young."

"Actually, he's our age."

"No, not in years, in life experience."

She nodded. "That could be. Though he's travelled everywhere, his parents dote on him. He always gets his way." She smirked. "Not this time."

Ryan cupped her cheek. "I don't care that you're pregnant. That little baby will be a part of you and that's all that matters. Lynzie, I love you."

Oh, my God! Her heart soared as he brought her face to his and kissed her gently. This couldn't be happening. No man was this amazing. She pulled back a little. "Are you sure?"

His ever-present grin returned. "I'm more than sure. I thought the love I had for you as a teenager was nothing more than puppy love. But I know now it was much more."

"Oh, Ryan. I love you so much!" She couldn't resist any longer and pulled him in for a kiss that showed him exactly how much she cared. He tasted of peppermint and smelled like the crisp outdoors after a snowfall.

He deepened the kiss, sweeping his tongue into her mouth and making her knees weak. His hand pressed her hard against him and she felt how much he wanted her. It was the final straw. She needed him.

# CHAPTER SEVEN

Lynzie pulled her mouth from Ryan's and started to unbutton his shirt.

He grasped her hand. "Are you sure?"

"I'm very sure. I've waited far too many years to show you how much you mean to me."

His brown eyes turned almost black as he searched her eyes for the truth. There was only one thing for him to see. Her absolute love for him. He lowered his mouth to her neck and kissed her there, sending a delightful shiver down her back.

"I'm going to show you exactly how special you are to me." Ryan's breath on her skin sent excitement racing through her, or was it his words?

He unclipped her hair at the back of her neck where she had pulled it together for work. Then his fingers moved beneath it and massaged her head.

"That feels so good."

"You feel so good." He stood and pulled her up with him, turning her so she faced the tree, her back to him.

She missed the warmth of his body, but when she felt him unbuttoning the back of her dress, she warmed up quickly. What would he think? It had been so long since he'd seen her.

He opened the dress and moved her hair aside, kissing her upper back, her shoulder, the nape of her neck, as if he worshipped her. It made her lightheaded and she widened her stance to keep herself upright.

Then her dress fell away and piled at her feet. She sucked in her breath as Ryan stepped against her and wrapped his arms about her bare waist, burying his face in her hair. In that instant, she felt herself in harmony with the world as if he was the piece that had been missing, keeping her off balance.

His hands moved, splaying over her trim tummy and down her abdomen. "You are going to make a wonderful mother."

Her heart filled with hope. She wanted to have *his* baby, a boy with his father's dark looks who could ride his pony at the age of five. The vision took her breath away.

Then Ryan's hands moved lower, cupping her, holding her to him.

She could feel his hardness against her butt, which revved her senses higher, knowing he wanted her as much as she wanted him. She moaned quietly, her body melting.

He brought his hands up and cupped her breasts in her peach-colored bra. She ached to feel him touch her there. As if he read her mind, he moved his fingers to the front clasp and opened it.

She sighed in anticipation as he pushed the cups aside. Finally his hands were on her, brushing over her sensitive peaks.

"You are so beautiful."

She grinned. "You can't even see me."

His head came away from her shoulder where he'd been kissing her skin and he turned her around.

She sucked in her breath as he stepped back and looked.

"You're right. Now I can see you far surpass 'beautiful.' You're heavenly."

Her whole body heated as his gaze swept over her. When he finally looked her in the eyes, she could see the love he had for her. "Please make love to me."

Ryan's eyes, so dark to start with, appeared to turn black at her words. He stepped toward her and swept her up into his arms.

She wrapped her arms around his neck and kissed him on the cheek before he brought them into her bedroom. As they passed the doorway, she flipped the switch, lighting it up the with a single string of colored Christmas lights.

He gently set her on her bed. The silky purple quilt felt decadent against her skin.

He stood back and unbuttoned his green flannel shirt. Then he shrugged it off.

She caught her breath. The muted light cast shadows over his chest and abs, making the muscle definition stand out even more.

Next he unbuttoned his jeans and toed off his boots. She held her breath as he unzipped his pants and pushed them down. Crap, his thigh muscles were huge! She felt an ache deep in her core. Quickly, she sat up, wiggled her bra straps off her shoulders.

She yanked off her boots and socks, leaving her in her peach-colored underwear. When she looked up from her task, she found Ryan gazing at her, his body completely naked, his own need for her obvious.

He gave her a hesitant smile as he turned sideways. "You should probably see this now."

In the Christmas-light glow, she could see a number of scars around his right hip. Some were long and had obviously been stitched, but others were jagged and angular. She reached out and brushed her fingers over them. At his intake of breath, she paused. "Do they hurt?"

He shook his head. "No. It's your touch. It makes me want to take you right now."

She removed her hand as heat raced to the juncture of her thighs. "Then do."

Ryan leaned over the bed and kissed her. His tongue took over and love gave way to passion. He knelt on the bed and pushed her back against the quilt, his weight covering her, his hard body pressing into her.

She welcomed him with open arms, grasping him to her as she pressed herself against him.

He left her mouth to trail a path of kisses down her body, starting with her breasts, across her belly button, and over her abdomen. Then he hooked his fingers in the elastic at her hips and pulled her panties off.

"Ah, Lynz. I want to go slow, but I can't wait to bury myself inside you."

She shook her head. "Please don't. I've needed you for over a decade. Don't make me wait."

He covered her with his body again. "Are you sure you're ready?"

She nodded. "I am."

He lifted his hips and stilled. "I don't want to hurt the baby. Is it okay?"

"Yes. The doc said it was fine." Her need was clawing at her. "Please."

Ryan positioned himself at her entrance. "Damn, I forgot to ask."

She grabbed hold of his arms. "I'm good. Part of my doctor's visit was testing for everything. I'm clean."

She felt the tension leave him. "Good. So am I."

Her entire body tensed, anxious for his penetration, and then he lowered his hips, slowly gliding into her.

"Yesss." The word came out on a sigh as he filled her.

Their hips stay joined as he kept from crushing her by leveraging himself on his elbows. "Lynz?"

She opened her eyes, not sure when she'd closed them. "Yes?"

His gaze was intense. "I'm going to make you mine now."

Her throat closed at the raw passion in his voice. She nodded.

At her agreement, his need showed on his face. It sent excitement barreling through her even as he lifted his hips and thrust.

Pleasure filled every space in her body.

Ryan took her mouth then, his tongue claiming her even as his body did the same, pumping into her faster and faster.

She met each thrust, the sensations inside her building, tightening, bringing her closer to fulfillment. Then Ryan's body stiffened and he held her against him as liquid fire filled her and her world exploded.

Love, passion, goodness collided inside, mixing together to blanket her in a peace she never knew existed.

She clung to him as her body calmed.

Ryan brushed her hair away from her face.

She opened her eyes and smiled. "I didn't know it could feel like that."

His grin returned. "Me neither."

She touched his face in wonder. "I guess it was meant to be."

He turned his head and kissed her palm. Then he cocked his head. "Do you hear that?"

She listened. The south church bells chimed a joyful melody. "Midnight Mass must be over."

He shook his head. "No. That's love causing the bells to chime."

"Ours?"

"Of course."

She laughed as pure happiness filled her.

Lynzie sat on the stool before the Christmas tree watching the lights, still amazed at how lucky she was.

Ryan leaned back against her. He still hadn't put his shirt back on, mainly because she didn't want him to. She could never grow tired of looking at those abdominals.

He tweaked her hat. "What are you thinking about?"

"I'm thinking about how lucky I am."

He smiled. "Funny, I was thinking the same thing."

She leaned over and kissed him on the cheek. "This is the best Christmas I've ever had."

"For me too. Not only did I discover the woman I love, loves me back, but I sold Lazy Acres."

"What?" She jumped off the stool and sat on the floor to face him. "That's wonderful! Was it that Scottish buyer? Did you get your asking price? Wait, you're just telling me this now?"

Ryan laughed. "I'm telling you this now because the most important part of my life had to come first."

"You're a sweet-talker Ryan Crawford. Now tell me all about it."

"I'm trying." He chuckled and pulled her onto his lap. "The foreign buyer didn't show. My real estate agent never heard from him, so she thinks he got cold feet. As it turns out, we had a developer come in the very next day and offer us our asking price."

"Wow. That's fantastic!"

He squeezed her. "But it gets even better."

"How can it get better than that?"

"We close December thirtieth. We'll be back at Broken Oak with Midnight and Toby by a week from Sunday."

Lynzie's heart stopped. "You close before New Year's?"

"Yes. Things couldn't have gone smoother."

She pulled out of his embrace and leaned her back against the couch. "But then you'll be gone and I'll be here." How could he have told her he loved her and made love to her when all along he knew he would leave. It was too cruel.

"Lynzie, not just me. *We.* I want you to come with me."

She shook her head. "But I can't leave Lucasville now."

Ryan's heart twisted around in his chest. "What do you mean you can't leave? Of course, you can. You can finally work with horses like you wanted, though there won't be a lot of training. And your mom is happily married, so you have no reason to stay. Don't you see, it's perfect."

She shook her head and crossed her arms over her stomach like she needed to protect the baby. "I can't leave. My baby needs a father."

His gut relaxed. "Lynz, I told you, I'll be your baby's father."

"I know you would, but I can't take the baby from his or her real dad. I was nine when I lost mine. Sure, Paul came around years later, but it's not the same."

"But if your baby doesn't know any dad but me, why would it make a difference. I'm telling you, I will love him or her as if they were my own."

Lynzie started to cry, wrenching his heart more. "But I'd know. And how can I deny Andrew the chance to know his child. It's just not right."

As much as he hated it, he couldn't deny her point. Though he thought Andrew would be a lousy dad, the man did have a right to know his own child. Fuck. "There's got to be a way we can make this work."

But she shook her head and deep down he knew that no matter what solution he suggested, visitation, summers, anything, she would knock it down for the baby's sake. He fisted his hands, frustrated beyond belief, but unable to do anything about it. "So where does that leave us?"

"I don't think we can have an *us*. I didn't realize you'd be leaving so soon."

He stood. "So you thought we could just see each other and when I left you'd wave goodbye. Do you realize how cruel *that* would have been? How cruel it is?"

She rose as well. "I didn't even think that far. I was too in love with you to care beyond tonight. It seemed that at long last things were going my way, but I can see that's not the case."

Despite the tears running down her face, he still wanted to shake her and make her think of another way. He didn't want to lose her again. "There's got to be a way we can do this."

"Unless you plan to sell your ranch and move back here, I don't see how it can work."

He grasped her by the shoulders. "Please, Lynzie. Think about it. There must be a solution."

She shook her head at him, telling him clearly that she wouldn't budge on anything. Despite the pain in his chest, he held her close for a moment and kissed her with all the love in his heart. Then without a word, he picked up his hat, shrugged into his shirt and walked to the door.

He looked back when she didn't ask him to stay only to find her staring at him, her tears still falling. The pain in his chest grew worse. Grabbing his coat off the hook, he slammed his hat on his head and left. The sound of the door closing sounded like a death knell to his heart.

He couldn't let this go. He would think of something when he was calmer, when he could be more pragmatic about it. And then he would bring the solution to Lynzie on a platter like she served drinks at the Pub.

Jumping in his truck, he turned the ignition and put it into drive. Looking up at her apartment, he could see the pink glow from the Christmas tree in her window. There had to be a way.

But as he drove out of the parking lot, his confidence slipped.

# CHAPTER EIGHT

L y.nzie Mullins?" At her name being called by the medical assistant, she rose.

"Do you want me to come with you?" Coco cocked her head.

"Of course. That's why I brought you." She grabbed Coco's hand and pulled her with her. She was scared. She shouldn't have any bleeding, but she did.

The assistant led them into a darkened room where she traded her sweater for a flimsy white paper cover then sat on the table to wait.

Coco, as usual, couldn't let them sit in silence. "Did you tell anyone else what's going on."

"No. I'm hoping there's nothing wrong. I just told my mom two days ago. She hasn't even had the chance to be happy yet. I'm a healthy adult. I've been having really bad morning sickness and getting sick when I'm hungry. My guess is something is out of balance."

"Are you taking those vitamins they told you about?"

"Of course." She was following Dr. Brady's

instructions to the letter. Ever since Christmas Eve night, she'd totally focused on her baby, determined to give it a wonderful life somehow.

When the ultrasound technician walked in and sat down, Coco sat beside her and held her hand. After a few minutes of rubbing cold jelly stuff over her abdomen with some kind of wand, the technician left without saying anything.

Coco stood up. "I don't think they're allowed to say anything until the doctor reads the results.

"That sounds right." But nothing seemed right, especially the jelly stuff she wiped off her body before putting her sweater back on.

Next they were shown to an exam room and they waited some more. A young woman came in. "Hi, Lynzie, I'm Danielle, Dr. Brady's physician assistant. I reviewed the result of your ultrasound and I'm afraid there is no heartbeat."

"What?" Coco's surprise didn't mirror her own.

Deep down she'd known something was wrong.

Danielle placed her hand on her arm. "I'm very sorry. You will probably miscarry in the next twenty-four hours. When you do, please bring it in and we will do a D and C."

Bring it in? Lynzie stared at the woman as if she'd lost her head, but she nodded mutely. No way would she do any of that.

After the physician assistant left, Coco led her

down the hall and outside. She stared blankly at the passersby, the usual speeding traffic and the swaying Christmas bunting on the place next door.

"Come on, Lynzie. Let's get you home and into bed. I'll call Lorenzo and let him know you won't be in tonight."

She followed Coco's instructions numbly, changing into her pajamas and crawling into bed even though it was still light outside.

"Try to get some sleep. I'll be back as soon as I get the shop closed up."

She nodded at her friend, too stunned to really comprehend what had happened. She heard the door to her apartment close, but didn't care. Her baby was no more. No, her baby was dead but still inside of her. How could this have happened? She did everything she was supposed to do. This wasn't supposed to happen.

Her tears started as the reality finally penetrated her heart. Now that it was gone, she wanted her baby more than ever.

Eventually, she cried herself to sleep. She woke once with cramps and found Coco sitting next to the bed. She ran and got her ibuprofen, but she refused it, falling back to sleep. In the middle of the night, she cried out as a sharp pain sliced through her abdomen. "Oh God."

She opened her eyes to find Coco at her bedside again. "Hey."

"Hey. How are you feeling?"

"Tired." She moved her arm out from under the covers to reach for the water Coco handed her and noticed she had on a different pair of pajamas. Images from the middle of the night flashed before her and she started to cry.

"Oh boy, I'm so sorry, Lynzie."

She nodded but kept crying her silent tears.

"Do you want me to tell anyone?"

"Could you tell my mom?"

"Of course. Who else knows?"

She handed back the water and snuggled under the covers, her tears still falling. "Just Ryan and Andrew. I'm going back to sleep." Maybe in her dreams she could forget the feeling of deep loss that seemed to permeate her soul.

⸻

Ryan watched as Gramps signed the last document. He'd been greatly relieved by the test results they'd received on his grandpa's condition. It was a vitamin deficiency.

Unfortunately, it was a severe vitamin deficiency and Gramps would have to undergo a series of daily shots. He would stay a little longer to be sure Gramps was on the road to recovery and taking his required pill when the shots were done.

Even then he'd come back to Lucasville and check

on him. It was a short plane ride from northern Florida and worth every penny to be sure his grandpa lived to a healthy old age. He still hoped to have him come to Broken Oak eventually.

Coming to Lucasville could give him a chance to check in on Lynzie as well. He just wasn't sure his heart could handle that. Since he still loved her, or loved her more, the thought of her living in Lucasville while he was in another state hurt more than the bullet that made mincemeat of his hip.

After congratulations were extended to everyone at the kitchen table, he walked out the real estate agent and the developer. He was happy for himself and Gramps, but the last thing the town needed was another development.

Maybe that was just him still holding on to the past. After the visitors drove away, he strolled around the house to look at the barn with its new boards that would no longer need painting since it would be bulldozed to the ground.

He gazed past that to the north pasture where Midnight and Toby trotted, loving the large area. At least he could give them a new home. They might even be able to help some of his future customers.

Now he needed to let Antony know he was done. His old high school friend wasn't going to be happy. He could keep working there another week, while Gramps got his shots, but then they had to leave the property.

Ryan cracked his neck, the stress of the upcoming conversation already stiffening him up. Best to get it over with sooner rather than later. With a heavy sigh, he turned and strode back into the house.

"Gramps, I'm going into town. Do you want to come?"

"Nah, I'm going up to take a nap. Don't know why they have to make all that writing so damn small. Makes my eyes tired."

He smiled fondly at his grandpa and touched him on the shoulder. "Are you happy with the sale?"

Gramps grinned. "Very." Then he frowned and waved his finger. "Don't you worry. I'll be cutting you a check just as soon as everything clears. You did good."

He shrugged. "I just hired the right real estate agent."

"No, you made the place look good, even if they're going to tear it down, it looks better now than it has for years. I'm proud of you."

"Thanks, Gramps." He gave his grandpa a hug then pulled back, knowing the man wasn't in to showing affection.

"Now go do what you have to do. I'm going to sleep." Gramps walked out of the kitchen.

Ryan listened to the old man climb the stairs. When he heard the creak of the floorboard beneath the bed, he grinned. He couldn't imagine sleeping in the middle of the day like that, but then again, he wouldn't be thirty until March. Maybe when he was in his seventies, he would want to do that.

Right now, however, he needed to quit his part-time job. Shrugging into his leather jacket, he donned his hat and headed for his truck. Once on the road, he swore people had forgotten all their Christmas spirit. He had to slam on his breaks twice to avoid hitting someone before he finally found parking not far from the Love garage.

He walked in and scanned the garage for Antony, but didn't see him. The place was packed with vehicles needing to be repaired. On one hand, he'd miss this, but on the other hand, he'd get to go back to fixing tractors and forklifts and all the other farm equipment he would have to buy used. The less he spent on machinery, the more he could spend on staff and horses.

He strode around the corner and knocked on Antony's office door.

"Come in."

He walked in to find Antony scowling at Aiden, his youngest brother.

"I can come back."

Antony shook his head. "No, come in. Aiden was just leaving."

Aiden gave him a shit-eating grin. "Yup. He's all yours."

Ryan never had a brother, so he never could understand what appeared to be a love/hate relationship between the Love brothers. He hadn't envied them that, but he had envied their relationship with Anton, their father.

"I guess you're here to quit on me." Antony leaned back in his chair, resigned to losing him.

"What makes you say that?"

"Maybe because you're here on your day off. Either that or you've decided you like this place so much you want to be here every day."

He smirked. "To tell the truth, I do like it here. You have a great shop and some very good mechanics, but you're right, I do have to quit. Lazy Acres sold."

Atony whistled between his teeth. "That was fast. Hope you got a good price."

He nodded. "Yeah, the asking price."

"Must be another developer." Antony frowned.

He did feel guilty about that, but if Gramps held out for a buyer who wanted a horse farm, it wouldn't have slowed the growth of the town by much. It had simply become *the* place to live.

"So how long before you leave?"

"Less than a week. I could probably give you a few more days."

"Good, I'll take it. We're slammed. Any chance you can work tomorrow?"

Ryan relaxed. He'd expected to be given a hard

time by Antony. "Gramps would have my head if I worked on a Sunday. I'll come in Monday afternoon."

"Great." Antony stood and held out his hand. "Congratulations. I'm glad you were able to sell the old place. If you ever come back to town, you can always work for me again."

He shook his friend's hand. "Thanks Antony."

The man nodded. "You going to see Lynzie before you leave?"

He should have known their relationship was a subject of conversation among his old high school peers. He decided to test the waters. "I've seen her a few times already."

"That's not what I mean. You know she was a mess after you left the first time."

He rubbed the back of his neck, his heart constricting. "Yeah, I know. I asked her to come with me."

"And…?"

He shook his head, not willing to get into it. "Let's just say it's not going to work out." It should have and he'd left her at least a dozen messages with ideas, but she didn't call back.

"Sorry about that."

"Yeah, me too."

# CHAPTER NINE

Lynzie waited outside the little bistro. It was cold but sunny and she'd much rather meet Andrew out here because the more she thought about telling him about the baby, the tighter her stomach became. She hadn't eaten much in the last few days anyway. Why she thought she could have Sunday brunch with him was beyond her.

Coco came outside. "Are you coming in or not?"

She shook her head.

"Okay, I'll tell them to release our table."

Her friend disappeared back inside. She was so lucky she had her. If it hadn't been for her and her mom, she would have never made it through the last few days.

She looked at the clock on the south church tower. Where was he? He was already twenty minutes late. It was almost noon. Lowering her gaze, she caught sight of him as he turned the corner. He waved, as if she wouldn't realize it was him.

When he reached her, he leaned down to kiss her,

but she turned her head so he kissed her cheek. "I'm glad you called. I think we have a lot to talk about. Are you ready for breakfast?" He looked down at her waist. "I mean, since you are eating for two now."

She couldn't pretend nothing was wrong. "I lost the baby."

At the look of shock on his face, she kicked herself for being so blunt, but her emotions were stretched to the max. "I'm sorry."

His surprise turned to skepticism. "Did you abort it like I suggested?"

"What?" Her anger bubbled up fast. "No, not at all. I wanted it."

He had the gall to smile. "I can understand that. After all, it was a piece of me you could call your own."

She stared at him in shock. Really?

"I have to tell you, I'm very relieved. We didn't need a baby between us. It's much better as it is."

"As it is?" She tried to understand him, but his thoughts were so far from her reality that she couldn't quite grasp them. "We don't have anything, Andrew."

"You mean because of that old flame of yours? I wouldn't hold out too much hope for him. His grandpa hates you. He'll never allow anything to happen there."

A niggling idea formed in her mind. "I never could understand that. He loved me when I was younger."

Andrew shook his head. "You need to listen to old timers more often. Don't you know that what you do with your life is the most important thing to them. You've done nothing. I just happened to drop a few hints about that in the hardware store the other day and the next thing I know you are person non-grata at that lazy farm place."

She took a step back toward the curb. "That was you? Why?"

Andrew looked around. "Let's go inside and discuss this over some warm food."

She shook her head. "No, I want to know right now. Why did you do that to me?"

He shrugged. "I didn't want you leaving town. This is where you belong. This is what you were born to. Besides, I didn't want to lose such an energetic bedmate." He had the audacity to wiggle his brows.

She shook her head at him and stepped back into the street between two parked cars. He was the devil incarnate or something.

Just then Coco came out. "So, you finally showed up."

Andrew looked at her. "What's it to you? I'm having a private conversation with Lynzie, if you don't mind?"

"Trust me, there's nothing private about it." Coco stepped between the parked cars. "Are you okay?"

Lynzie couldn't take her eyes of the man on the sidewalk. Had she really slept with him?

"Listen Lynzie." Andrew took a step closer.

Since you're good now, do you want to get together tonight?"

Oh, my God! She took two steps back, needing to get away from him.

Car brakes squealed.

Ryan parked his truck on a side street and jumped out. He called himself twice a fool for being unable to leave town without seeing Lynzie one more time. It may be a lost cause, but he had to try to convince her to come with him.

He fingered the piece of paper in his pocket with his name, phone number, and the address to Broken Oak Farm. That was his safety net. If she refused again, he'd give her his information in the hope she'd contact him eventually. He needed that hope.

He turned the corner on to Main Street and looked down the sidewalk. If she was out and about, he didn't want to miss her. People jostled him as they walked by and then there was no one in front of him.

Four storefronts down he saw Andrew talking to someone by the parked cars. Ryan's gaze switched to that spot and Ryan saw Coco and her tell-tale pink streak of hair. Past her, stepping out into the street, was Lynzie.

No! His heart leapt into his throat as he started to run. Everything seemed like slow motion, even his own movements.

Car brakes squealed as a vehicle headed straight for Lynzie. She turned her head to see it and then she was down.

He ran into the street to find her on the ground and alive, but Coco thrown half way between him and the woman he loved.

Lynzie screamed and ran to Coco even as he got there.

"Oh, my God. Coco. What did you do?"

Coco opened her eyes. "You're okay."

Lynzie knelt beside her friend. "I am, thanks to you."

"I wasn't sure if I should push or pull. I was afraid you'd resist if I tried to pull you back in, so I pushed. Guess I should have pulled." Coco coughed.

"You're going be all right." Lynzie looked up at him begging him with her eyes to agree with her.

He'd seen many wounded overseas, enough to know that Coco wasn't going to make it. He shook his head slightly, hating to break her heart, but if these were the last seconds she had with her friend, he wanted her to have them.

Tears streamed down her face even as she smiled at Coco. "Just hang on until the ambulance arrives."

Coco glanced at him then back to Lynzie and smiled. "Lynz, he's your soulmate."

Lynzie's eyes found his in a quick glance before

she returned her gaze to her friend. She held Coco's hand. "He is?"

"Yes, and you must do whatever you have to in order to stay with him. Promise me."

Lynzie nodded. "I promise, but only if you get better."

"No! Promise. You must be together. I can see it. Promise me." Coco's voice sounded panicked.

Lynzie's voice came out in barely a whisper. "I promise."

Coco's eyes closed. "Good. Wear the white gown for your wedding. It will be perfect."

As Lynzie nodded, Coco breathed her last breath.

"No." She squeezed Coco's hand. "Not you, too. Please."

The south church bells chimed to signal mass had let out. Their joyous music seemed to herald a new soul in their midst. Then they were drowned out by the siren of the ambulance.

Ryan's heart hurt for Lynzie. He wanted to blame someone, anyone. He looked at the car, but no one was in it. He scanned the gathered crowd and found Andrew. Every ounce of fury in him found its target.

He parted the crowd and grabbed Andrew by the throat and pushed him against the wall of the bistro.

"Hey, what are you doing? You're hurting me."

"That's nothing compared to the pain Lynzie is

feeling right now. I think you need to feel what Coco feels."

Andrew's eyes widened as he clawed at his wrists.

Gramps came from somewhere and pulled at his right arm. "Ryan, let him go. Harvey, help me. I don't want my grandson in jail. Not for this man."

Ryan felt someone pulling on his left arm too, making it hard to keep his hold.

"Ryan, son, let him go. He's not worth you going to jail."

He moved his gaze to his grandpa's voice and relaxed his hands. Andrew fell to his knees taking in deep breaths.

"Go to your girl. She needs you now."

He looked blindly at Gramps, his rage slowly dissipating.

Andrew stood, still rubbing at his throat. "You think I'm not worth it?" His voice was scratchy, barely audible. "Lynzie's not worth it."

Before anyone could stop him, he swung his fist and knocked Andrew out. Then he turned on his heel, parting the crowd to get to Lynzie. She still knelt on the road, shaking her head, unwilling to move though Coco's body had already been loaded into the ambulance.

"Lynz."

At his voice, she looked up at him with such sorrow, it closed his throat. He opened his arms and she threw herself into them, sobbing so hard, she shook them both. As the paramedics cleared the scene and the police cordoned it off, he held her, keeping the official at bay with a look.

When her sobs quieted to just crying, he lifted her in his arms and walked to the sidewalk.

A policeman stopped him. "We'll need to ask you both a few questions."

He swallowed hard to get his throat to work. "Fine. We'll be at Lazy Acres farm." Then he walked by and headed for his truck.

<hr>

Lynzie walked away from the burial site, her arm around Ryan's waist. "It was my fault. If I hadn't stepped out in to the street, she'd still be alive."

"I know you feel that way, but we can just as easily blame Andrew for being such a worthless human being that you needed to get away from him, and it still wouldn't bring her back."

She sighed. "I know that in my head, but my heart keeps telling me it was my fault. I was the one who should have been hit." She felt a shiver race through Ryan's body. "I'm sorry. I know you hate to hear that."

He stopped them in front of his truck and turned her to face him. "I do hate to hear that because then I would have lost you forever. You have to remember that Coco *chose* to save you. She loved you like a sister.

Your friendship is very special. She is truly your guardian angel, more so now than ever before."

She gazed into his dark eyes and finally his words penetrated her heart. Tilting her head, she looked up at the sky. "Thank you, Coco." She met his gaze again. "And thank you for saying that our friendship is still alive. I do feel that."

He pulled her in to an embrace, and she rested her face against his chest. Wherever Coco was, singing with the angels or dancing in a pink gown like the one she never got to wear, Lynzie promised to make her proud. She would make every second of her life count, just like Ryan had told her and Coco had showed her.

# EPILOGUE

$L$ynzie laughed as Ryan swept her up into his arms and opened the door to the big house of Broken Oak Farm. "Ryan, we already did this during the honeymoon."

He shook his head. "That doesn't count. This is your home now so I must carry you across the threshold."

She tweaked his cowboy hat as he brought her inside. Then the large beams above her caught her attention, and she looked around her. "Wow, this place is huge."

"Welcome home, Mrs. Crawford." He let her feet down and helped her stand.

She turned and faced him. "I'll never tire of hearing myself called that."

"Called what?" The deep voice came from behind Ryan, and she peeked around him. A very large man stood staring at them. He had to be at least six feet six and he looked about four feet wide. His buzz cut proclaimed him a veteran. There was only one male friend of Ryan's who lived at Broken Oak.

Despite his scary appearance, she stepped around her new husband. "I'm guessing you're Cooper."

The large man cracked a small smile. "That I am, Ma'am. Welcome to the Broken Oak."

"Thank you. I understand you've been taking care of the place. That seems like a big job."

"I'm a big man." The words were said with pride.

"Yes, you are." She held out her hand. "Hi, I'm Lynzie."

Cooper shook her hand. "I'm glad you married this guy." He looked over her shoulder at Ryan. "He needs someone else to watch over him."

"Easy." Ryan placed his hands on her shoulders. "I'm really not that hard to look after." He spoke to Cooper. "Where's Jessie?"

He pointed over his shoulder. "She was stacking hay last I saw her."

"I'm here. The grizzly bear here couldn't wait for his partner to get down from the hayloft. Instead, he had to come running to greet you." A tall woman in an Army t-shirt and fatigue pants stepped forward awkwardly and held out her hand. "Hi, I'm Jessie. I served with Ryan in Afghanistan."

"It's a pleasure to meet you. I'm Lynzie."

"Is there any chance you know how to cook? I really suck at it and these two gorillas think I'm supposed to be genetically disposed to it."

Lynzie gave her a crooked smile. "I can do a few

things, but I can always ask my mom for help if I need it."

Jessie looked away. "That's good. We can use all the help we can get."

Cooper gestured over his shoulder. "I don't see your grandpa. Does he need help getting inside?"

Ryan shook his head. "No, he's not coming, at least not yet. He's settling into his new condo with the swimming pool below. I think he's going to enjoy that place so much he may forget to visit Harvey."

Lynzie turned her head to look back at him. "Why do you say that?"

He chuckled. "I saw the old man buying binoculars."

Jessie shook her head but Cooper chuckled. "I look forward to meeting him."

Ryan pulled her back against him. "Okay, my new bride has had a long trip, so if you two don't mind, I'm going to give her the tour. Then I'm ordering pizzas so no one has to cook."

"Make sure you order me the all meat one." Cooper frowned. "I don't need any of those girly vegetables."

Jessie rolled her eyes at Cooper before walking by him. "Come on Major Meat, let's finish stacking that hay before it gets dark."

Cooper saluted behind Jessie's back before marching outside.

Lynzie turned in Ryan's arms. "I like them."

"I knew you would." He took her straw cowboy hat off and brushed her hair back. "The next few months will be a lot of work, so if it ever feels like I'm ignoring you, just tell me. I want you to be happy here."

She looped her arms around his neck. "You don't have to worry. As long as you are here, I'll love it. I don't want to spend any more time separated from you."

He grinned, his white teeth gleaming. "Good. Because we have five more horses to get settled in, staff to interview, and veteran's organizations to contact.

She laughed, thrilled to be a part of such an amazing project with such a wonderful man. "And don't forget lots of children."

He lowered his head and kissed her on the nose. "What do you say we get working on that right away."

She pretended to think about it. "Hmm, I don't know. We need to unpack and arrange the—"

He swept her back up into his arms and strode toward the stairs.

"Ryan, I'm too heavy. Let me down."

"Sorry Mrs. Crawford. You have a wifely duty to attend to first, and it appears the only way to make that happen is to bring you to the bedroom myself."

She giggled. "And what wifely duty would that be, Mr. Crawford?"

He pushed open the bedroom door and dropped

her on the bed. "I believe making love is your number one duty."

She scrambled up on her knees and began to unbutton his shirt. "Oh good. Now that is something I know I can do well."

*The End*

For updates, sneak peeks, and special prizes, sign up to receive the latest news from Lexi at https://app. mailerlite.com/webforms/landing/c1w1g3

*Read on for an excerpt of Desires of Christmas Present (A Christmas Carol #2)*

*A*rrogant. *Asshole.*

Those were the only two words that came to mind when Coco Baker heard the name, Ian Fergusson. Taken separately or together, they described him to a tee. "I'm sorry, but there's no way I can work with Ian Fergusson." She gripped the back of the chair in front of her. The man pissed her off simply by existing.

She didn't know how he'd ever been chosen as a spirit guide. She couldn't believe that the Scottish snob had ever had to work a day in his life. From what she'd seen, he didn't get along with any of the other spirit guides…or other spirits for that matter. Telling live people how they should feel and act just didn't work, and she was positive that's how he did his job.

Cameron Douglas, her boss, shook his head, his sandy brown hair falling onto his forehead with the movement. "I need two of you on this case. It's too hard a task for just one."

Oh, that was fine. "I can work with someone else, or if you like, I can bow out and wait for the next case." She'd just have to make it up to whoever was unlucky enough to be assigned to work with Ian.

Cameron leaned forward, setting his large arms on his desk and clasping his hands in front of him. "I'm afraid I need you, in particular, on this case."

"Me?" Had he noticed her track record? She'd begun to think only the spirits who knew spirits ever got promoted.

"Yes, you. I need your special instinct."

She flushed. "You know about that?"

"I do. It's nothing to be ashamed of, and on this assignment, it will be very important."

She dropped into the chair in front of her boss's desk. When she became a spirit, she was surprised to discover her ability to recognize soulmates was still with her, but only among the living. It had helped her succeed on more than one case, but it felt as if she cheated when she used it. "Does this assignment have to do with helping someone find their true love?"

"No. I'll explain as soon as Ian arrives."

Despite her dislike of the man, she looked forward to seeing him. It was a pity he was such an ass because his body was to die for. Not that she'd seen him in anything but nice clothes. Casual for that man was a polo shirt and slacks, but his broad shoulders, narrow waist and rounded ass filled it all out quite nicely.

She preferred casual, especially the flutter shirt she wore. The pink stripes went with the streak in her hair and the three-quarter, wide sleeves hid what she considered her large upper arms.

Cameron shifted in his seat, obviously growing impatient.

She didn't like uncomfortable silences, especially

with her boss. "Since we're waiting, could you tell me if Mrs. Maxwell is doing any better? I know I helped her see that she could still celebrate Christmas even though she was in a wheelchair, but I didn't run into Joy since she got back. Did all go as planned?"

Cameron relaxed, his smile quick. "Mrs. Maxwell is doing very well. The three of you did an excellent job with her."

She'd really liked the old widow and could see that her true soulmate had passed away. It hadn't been easy finding the right people to visit so Mrs. Maxwell could see she still had a purpose in life and a reason to live. "I'm glad. That woman has so much love to give, it would be a pity for it to end too soon. I think mankind needs as many people like her as it can get."

"I agree." Cameron sighed. "Unfortunately, Christmas can be the time of year when those very people find it the most difficult to keep going."

Boy, he could say that again. She'd seen far too many cases like Mrs. Maxwell's since she'd become a spirit guide.

—

Ian held Lucy's tiny hand firmly as he flew them over the rooftops of Glasgow, her silence an oddity after all her chattering this night. When they landed back in her bedroom, he let go and knelt in front of her. "Do you understand now?"

The eight-year-old nodded. "I do. Thank you for showing me. I promise I will be strong and not let anyone bully me into thinking I'm worthless." She pressed her finger against her chest. "I'm worth a million pounds!"

He smiled. "That's right. And what about the bullies?"

Her wide smile dimmed. "I feel sorry for them. I didn't know."

"Come here." He opened his arms wide and Lucy stepped into them. Hugging her was a balm for his soul that wouldn't last, but he craved it nonetheless.

Her pudgy little arms finally released him, and there was a tear in her eye.

"Now, Pumpkin. No weeping. Remember you still have another visitor coming tonight."

Her face brightened immediately. "Will he be as braw as you?"

Ian chuckled. "I don't know. It could very well be a woman who can talk dresses and dolls with you."

"I want a braw man." She crossed her arms over her chest and frowned at him.

He lowered his brow. "Now Lucy, remember what I said about how special you are. You don't want me to cancel the next spirit altogether, do you?"

Her eyes widened. "Oh, no." She grabbed his arm. "Please let the spirit come."

He kissed her on the tip of her nose before rising

to his full height. "All right, Pumpkin. I'll send the next spirit. Now let's return you to normal."

She stood still with her arms wide. "I'm ready."

He placed his hand on her shoulder and unphased her, his physical connection with her at an end. "Now you crawl into bed and take a nap." He glanced at the clock. "Your next visitor will be here in an hour and you want to be fresh for your trip into the future."

She smiled and ran to her small bed. Scrambling into it, she pulled the covers up to her chin. "Can you kiss me goodbye?"

His heart swelled. "Of course." If it wasn't for his assignments, he probably would have faded into nothingness, like he'd heard some spirits had done.

Brushing Lucy's cheek with his hand, though she couldn't feel it, he bent and kissed her there.

"And this one." She turned her head and pointed to her other cheek.

He obediently kissed the other one.

"And here." She pointed to her nose and he chuckled.

"Okay, last one." He kissed her button nose. "Happy dreams."

She nodded and waved. "Bye."

He floated toward her ceiling and waved back.

Once above the roof, he headed for his supervisor's office, the warmth and peace of Lucy leaving him the faster he flew. A tiny flicker of hope remained, his craving for another case already urging him on.

With no time in the afterlife, he was outside Cameron's door in a moment. Opening it, he stepped inside.

Coco turned around in her chair. Ian Fergusson stood just inside the door. His tall, broad-shouldered physique looked hard beneath his golf shirt even while relaxed. His face was equally hard as were his steel grey eyes. His angular jaw and sharp nose with a slight hook downward would have been enough to warn anyone to stay away, and beneath his short red hair were equally sharp ears. Everything about him was unrelenting.

He looked down his nose at her before raising his gaze to Cameron who had stood at his entrance. "I was informed that you needed me for a case. I can come back when you're done."

Her boss held out his hand and smiled. "No, come in. You'll be working with Coco on this one."

Ian raised an eyebrow and strode forward to clasp Cameron's hand. "I was unaware you ever sent two spirit guides on one case. I have always worked alone. I complete my assignment successfully that way."

Cameron nodded as he sat again. "Please." He motioned toward the other chair.

"I'm good." Ian waved him off.

Coco gritted her teeth. That was so like him. He thought he was above them all and could do what he wanted. She turned her gaze to Cameron. "Why do you need two of us?"

Ian frowned. "Yes. I can't imagine a case so difficult that it takes two spirit guides."

A team player he was not, but she'd already known that.

Cameron studied her, then Ian. When his gaze drifted between them, it was obvious that whatever he was about to say was important. Finally, he spoke, but didn't make eye contact with either of them. "Your case is my wife."

Shocked, she sat forward in her chair. "Your wife? But I thought—"

Ian interrupted her. "I was of the understanding that we were not allowed to take assignments directly related to us."

Cameron's gaze moved to Ian. "We aren't. However, this case has been given approval by Remiel."

"I didn't realize special dispensation was possible."

Seriously? She swallowed an exasperated sigh. "That's exactly what Cameron just said." Dimwit. She shook her head at Ian.

He didn't even acknowledge her, his gaze riveted to Cameron.

Her boss stared Ian down, which gave her a

certain amount of satisfaction. Cameron's voice was hard. "This is a unique circumstance, Ian."

Her new "partner" had the grace to back down. Shoot, how was she going to control him if he tried pulling that crap on her? Maybe she needed to channel Cameron's deep tones.

The silence grew awkward so she jumped in. "What can we do for your wife?"

Cameron finally stopped glowering at Ian. Maybe he didn't like her partner either. That had to suck to not like your own employee. When she was alive, she had times when just being nice to her fellow workers was tough.

"Holly has stopped her deep mourning thanks to the spirit guides I sent to her last Christmas, but she has failed to join the living. She goes to work and does her errands, but beyond that, she stays by herself. It's become worse with the Christmas season." Cameron paused. "It's critical that she begin to socialize again."

Ian nodded, but Coco wanted more. "If your wife has stopped her mourning, why is she not socializing? Do you know? That might help us with our approach."

"I believe it's because she doesn't want to intrude on other people's lives. She thinks everyone else has the perfect life. Also, people who have come into our shop have shown her pity and she hates that."

Coco could hear the pride in Cameron's voice. Rumors around the lounge had it that Cameron and

Holly had one of those rare loves that only happen to one in a hundred couples. She'd seen many perfectly matched couples both while alive and in her new existence. If what her boss and his wife had once had was even better than that then she would do whatever it took to help Holly.

She glanced at Ian. He remained absolutely still, staring at Cameron. Did the man have no reaction? No feelings? His appearance seemed to grow more distinct, intense. She blinked. Nope. He was still a hard statue.

When she looked back at her boss, he was studying her, but he quickly moved his attention to Ian. "Do you have any questions?"

"Yes, one." He paused and spared her a brief look. "If you have Coco, who is quite capable of handling a case, then why do you need me to accompany her?"

Her mouth dropped open in astonishment. Was that a compliment from "Mr. Holier Than Thou"? The man did nothing but argue with her about anything and everything when they came into accidental contact with each other. Now he complimented her?

Cameron's mouth had opened and closed a couple times before he gave voice to his thoughts. "Coco, if you wouldn't mind, I'd like to talk to Ian alone."

She rose. "Of course. I'll drop in and see how Holly is." She looked at Ian. "If you are still on the case, just find me when you're ready."

"He will still be on the case." Cameron's hard tone sent a shiver down her spine. He was an easy going boss, not like her last one, but he did have a certain tone that made a person want to hightail it out of his office.

"Great." She didn't mean the word in any way, but she also didn't want to piss off Cameron. Phasing, she floated down through the floor, anxious to meet the woman who had captured her boss's heart.

*Desires of Christmas Present*

Read on for an excerpt of *Poisoned Honor (Broken Valor #2)*

# Chapter One

Tyler Adams heard the snap above him as the cable he held beneath the MH-65 Dolphin helicopter lost its tension and he plummeted toward the raging ocean.

*Fuck. He was too high!*

Fear shot through him, causing his heart to skip as adrenaline flooded his body. With the rush of energy, his brain clicked into action. *Survive. What do I need to do to survive?*

It hadn't been the first time his life had been threatened and his training kicked in. He looked down at the fast-approaching waves.

*Bend at the waist. Shit, no time!*

His body made contact, but it didn't feel like water, it felt like concrete as his knees gave way at impact. There was a blissful instance of nothing as he plunged beneath the surface and then pain exploded inside him.

"Arrggghhh!"

Tyler sat up in bed. Sweat coated his body. "Fucking goddamn nightmare." He rubbed his legs, the remembered agony of contact too real for any sane person. He wiggled his toes first to reassure himself they worked then bent his knees and threw his legs over the side of the bed.

Letting his head drop, he ran his hand through his short hair. Would he have these dreams forever? It had been four months since the accident. Why wouldn't they stop?

*You have unresolved emotions.*

The voice of the shrink he secretly went to hammered against his brain. He had only a week before he returned to regular duty. No one knew how much he dreaded that. How the fuck was he supposed to continue as a rescue swimmer when he'd woken in the hospital with a sudden fear of heights?

He glanced at the clock. 05:00. Today was his day off and he had an appointment with the shrink at 09:00. Maybe he could distract him, keep him from asking if he had the nightmare again. At least he'd convinced the Chief that he was fine, otherwise the government-contracted psychologist would never let him return to work.

Dr. Meghan Haskell was the one everyone was required to see if they needed help. He'd met her three weeks back when he'd given Drew a ride because it was raining. The kid didn't like getting wet and never wore a helmet while riding his foreign motorcycle.

He had the chance to see Meghan three more times, and every time he left he was glad she wasn't his shrink. There was no way he could tell her his issue. He'd be far too distracted.

Dr. Haskell was his age and stunning in a smart way. He always had a thing for gorgeous women in glasses. And she definitely qualified, grade A all the way. She dressed in a suit with a modest skirt, which showed off her toned legs in the high heels she wore. Her blouse was always demurely buttoned, but the profile of her suitcoat made it clear she had perfect curves.

It wasn't her beautiful body though that had him thinking about her more than he should. It was her eyes. They were a unique mixture of blue and green and they caught everything, his body movements, his tension, even his mannerisms.

That combined with her unique scent had his body paying attention. It was something citrus and spicy, like the tea she had in her hand last time he saw her.

She was always polite, giving him a smile. Class-act was written all over her, and he had every intention of asking her out *after* he returned to duty. There was no way he'd get closer to her beforehand. The last thing he needed was for her to figure out he was afraid of heights and tell his chief.

Even as he thought about her, his body started to respond, which was a lot better than how it felt a few minutes earlier. What he needed was a quick two-mile swim and three-mile run to help him shake off the vestiges of the nightmare. Standing, he stretched his arms upward, pulling at the knots in his back, more remnants from his accident.

He'd been lucky with a just a couple broken legs. Alix Buchanan had it a lot worse. He still couldn't believe Alix was paralyzed from the waist down after her accident last week. Flying helicopters was her life. Her expert maneuvering of the out-of-control copter had saved the lives of everyone on board.

There had been so many freak accidents at the Station in the last six months that some of the crew members said it was haunted. Even Kolbe, Alix's copilot, had started researching the ownership of the land to make sure it wasn't located on an old Native American burial ground.

Moving forward, Tyler limped toward his bathroom, his awkward gait pissing him off. As the hot water sluiced over his muscles, his body rearranged itself in to better working order.

He grabbed the soap. Too bad he couldn't trade his nightmares for hot dreams of Dr. Meghan Haskell. He couldn't quite read her. Sometimes he thought she might be interested and other times not so much.

Maybe that was another aspect that attracted him, her poise. She always seemed so together. As a rescue swimmer, he rarely had the chance to see that. Any women he saved were either panicked or in shock though for good reason.

No matter why or how much he was attracted to the doctor, he refused to do anything about it until he was back on regular duty and had kicked his stupid fear to the curb.

Rinsing off, he let the heat of the water sooth his still healing body. He wanted to get back to saving lives. It was what he did and in another week or so, ready or not, he would return to hanging from a hovering helicopter above the waves. *Way* above the waves.

Dr. Meghan Haskell hit "save" after jotting down a few notes on her last client and closed the file. She had five minutes before her eight o'clock appointment. She might as well have another shot of caffeine.

She stood and walked across the fake oriental carpet to her cabinet. Opening it, she poured boiling hot water from her electric tea kettle over a new teabag and watched it steep.

She'd never been a morning person, but the government contract for psychological services she'd won required her to be available starting at six in the morning. The powers-that-be wanted their military personnel in the right frame of mind for duty. Luckily, she didn't have a 6:00AM today, but the number of Coast Guard men and women coming in had begun to concern her.

Picking up her mug, she walked back to her

desk. She wasn't complaining about the increase in clients. In fact, the contract had given her a credibility in the community that she had lacked as the newest psychologist to open up shop in Crystal Waters.

She took a sip of ginger-lemon tea and closed her eyes. Hmm, she loved the scent and taste of it, soothing while stimulating. Opening her eyes, she clicked her calendar open on her laptop. Lifting the mug to her lips as she scanned who she should expect next, she paused, the spicy aroma teasing her nose. It was Drew Linden.

He'd been coming to her the longest of any of the Coast Guard personnel. That man loved to talk, which made her job easy for a change. Her other Coast Guard male clients made her feel like she was pulling teeth with no anesthetic. On the other hand, those same males had completed their sessions. This young man, and he was young, really had no specific issues from his accident, but it was clear he wanted a sympathetic ear. That she could do.

Besides, it was the man who gave Drew a ride on rainy days that made her tingle. She glanced out the window. It was gloomy and wet, but it didn't look like it was actually raining. Would Tyler come? He always came up to the reception area when he could as easily just drop Drew off at the door. She liked to think he enjoyed talking to her, but he was so polite, it could just be that he wanted to be sure Drew made his appointment on time, since Drew had a tendency to flirt with the receptionist.

Even as she took another sip of what was soothing tea a moment ago, her body heated with anticipation. Tyler was the first man she'd ever met who wasn't a lawyer or architect or other professional, and she was seriously attracted to him. Not just because of his stature, but with his smile, his looks, and his big heart. She'd learned a bit about the man since Drew started coming to see her a month ago.

Tyler looked far younger than his years. She figured he had to be about twenty-eight based on the clues Drew dropped. She wouldn't be surprised if Tyler was still carded for alcohol. His blond hair was cut short, shaved at the base and sides, but a little longer on top. She itched to run her fingers through it like he often did.

As for his broad shoulders, that was the only part of him she was sure about since Coast Guard crews at Air Station Crystal Waters were required to wear their flight suits on duty, and Tyler Adams filled his out well. The loose jumpsuit hid his body except for his shoulders.

If she ever ran into him in a grocery store or at the mall when he was out of uniform, she doubted she could get three words past her lips. For someone with a doctorate in psychology, she could barely focus when he was around.

He had a strong jaw line with just a hint of a cleft in his chin. When she wasn't looking into his gray eyes, she caught herself watching his very kissable lips. Unfortunately, they'd only had a few short conversations. She wanted to know the man.

Not everyone was cut out to be a rescue swimmer both physically and emotionally. Plus, the fact that he wasn't sent to her after what Drew described as a horrifying accident had her heart fluttering. He must have nerves of steel.

Male laugher outside the building had her setting her tea on her desk then moving closer to the window. Oh crap. She was just in time to see Tyler smile at Drew and give him a friendly punch in the arm. That smile alone was enough to fluster her, but Tyler wasn't in uniform. She watched the two men until they disappeared under the awning, her forehead pressed against the glass.

Stepping away, she took a couple deep calming breaths. She'd been taught to always play it cool, let the other person reveal what they would, but being around Tyler left her breathless. Now he'd be in the reception area any second and she'd have to contend with him in a pair of shorts and a t-shirt up close. Even from the window, with her glasses on, she could see the bulge of his calves two flights up.

"Pull yourself together, Meg. He's just a great looking, heroic man. He'll never ask you out if you slobber all over him." Hearing her own voice helped, and she took one more sip of tea to help slow her pulse then strode to her door.

She paused and straightened her suitcoat. Drew often flirted with the shared office secretary outside, which always gave her a few moments with Tyler. A question about what he would do on his day off seemed the best way to start the conversation. She always liked to be prepared.

Opening the door, she walked out into the reception area and waited.

*Poisoned Honor (Broken Valor Book 2)*

# ALSO BY LEXI POST

**Military Romance**

When Love Chimes
(Broken Valor: Book 1)
Poisoned Honor
(Broken Valor: Book 2)

**Contemporary Cowboy Romance**

Cowboys Never Fold
(Poker Flat Series: Book 1)
Cowboy's Match
(Poker Flat Series: Book 2)
Cowboy's Best Shot
(Poker Flat Series: Book 3)
Cowboy's Break
(Poker Flat Series: Book 4)

Christmas with Angel
(Last Chance Series: Book 1)
Trace's Trouble
(Last Chance Series: Book 2)

Fletcher's Flame
(Last Chance: Book 3)
Logan's Luck
(Last Chance Series: Book 4) *Coming 2017*

## Paranormal Romance

Masque
Passion's Poison
Passion of Sleepy Hollow
Pleasures of Christmas Past
(A Christmas Carol Series: Book 1)
Desires of Christmas Present
(A Christmas Carol Series: Book 2)
Temptations of Christmas Future
(A Christmas Carol: Book 3) *Coming 2017*

## Sci-fi Romance

Cruise into Eden
(The Eden Series: Book 1)
Unexpected Eden
(The Eden Series: Book 2) )
Eden Discovered
(The Eden Series: Book 3)
Eden Revealed
(The Eden Series: Book 4) *Coming 2017*

# ABOUT THE AUTHOR

Lexi Post is a New York Times and USA Today best-selling author of romance inspired by the classics. She spent years in higher education taking and teaching courses about the classical literature she loved. From Edgar Allan Poe's short story "The Masque of the Red Death" to Tolstoy's *War and Peace*, she's read, studied, and taught wonderful classics.

But Lexi's first love is romance novels. In an effort to marry her two first loves, she started writing romance inspired by the classics and found she loved it. From hot paranormals to sizzling cowboys to hunks from out of this world, Lexi provides a sensuous experience with a "whole lotta story."

Lexi is living her own happily ever after with her husband and her cat in Florida. She makes her own ice cream every weekend, loves bright colors, and you will never see her without a hat.

www.lexipostbooks.com